BRIAN

Jeremy Cooper is a writer and art historian, author of six previous novels and several works of non-fiction, including the standard work on nineteenth century furniture, studies of young British artists in the 1990s, and, in 2019, the British Museum's catalogue of artists' postcards. Early on he appeared in the first twenty-four of BBC's *Antiques Roadshow* and, in 2018, won the first Fitzcarraldo Editions Novel Prize for *Ash before Oak*.

'I don't think I've ever felt such warmth for a character, or that I've been able to see cinema through another's eyes in such a lucid, sustained way. As Brian moves further and further into a life of moviegoing, ordering his days, and then years, around it, he finds companionship and a calm sense of wellbeing. As I read this beautifully subtle novel, I found the same.'
— Amina Cain, author of *A Horse at Night*

'After having published his luminous *Ash before Oak*, Jeremy Cooper now brings us *Brian*, equally a work of mysterious interiority and poetry. It confirms that however solitary life might be, art enriches both our imaginations and our realities. This is a very tender book.'
— Xiaolu Guo, author of *A Lover's Discourse*

'What makes Jeremy Cooper's seventh novel appealing and convincing is the author's serene prose and tender, understated empathy.... This is an affectionate, thoughtful portrait of a gentle soul.'
— David Collard, *Times Literary Supplement*

'*Brian* is affecting, funny and, at 184 pages, a skilfully compressed chronicle of one man's life and the cornucopia of film that enriches it.'
— Max Liu, *Financial Times*

Praise for *Bolt from the Blue*

'There's a strange magic to Jeremy Cooper's writing. The way he puts words together creates an incantatory effect. Reading him is to be spellbound, then. I have no idea how he does it, only that I am seduced.'
— Ben Myers, author of *The Offing*

Praise for *Ash before Oak*

'Low-key and understated, this beautiful book ... is a civilized and melancholy document that slowly progresses towards a sense of enduring, going onwards, and even new life. It feels like a healing experience.'
— Phil Baker, *The Sunday Times*

'[W]hat Cooper offers, very boldly and successfully, is a broad narrative arc of collapse and tentative recovery, in which a struggle for meaning and purpose in life assumes a desperate intensity.... Because of the narrator's inability to describe his anguish, what's mostly written here is not his pain, but his clinging to life: the beauty caught and traced, with great skill, in trying to overcome suffering. In its journal form, *Ash before Oak* salvages detritus, the unremarkable mess, banality and repetition of the everyday, just as the narrator works on restoring his dilapidated buildings in Somerset. And in a larger way, too, with admirable wisdom and precision, it salvages, from agonizing, ruinous thoughts and experiences, something transcendent, of lasting value.'
— Jerome Boyd Maunsell, *Times Literary Supplement*

'A disarming and gorgeously rendered portrait of interiority... The novel's genius lies in what goes unsaid, and in the gaps between entries – what the narrator keeps from readers is the most haunting plot of all. This meandering novel is one of quiet beauty, and brief flashes of joy among seasons of despair. A study in how writing can give lives meaning, and in how it can fail to be enough to keep one afloat, this is a rare, delicate book, teeming with the stuff of real life.'
— *Publishers Weekly*, starred review

Fitzcarraldo Editions

BRIAN

JEREMY COOPER

Brian became a regular at the BFI in stages. He did everything carefully, testing the water up and down the beach before taking the occasional swim. Prior to this big change in his life, he had gone to the movies casually, half a dozen times a year, maybe more, to the cinema nearest to wherever he was living. Though Brian was keen on film, his nervous concern focused on work, on holding down his job, leaving little energy for anything else, content to spend most evenings in front of the television with a mug of tea and packet of Chocolate Creams, his favourite biscuit. Without knowing quite why, or needing to find out, since missing its release a decade earlier he had always wanted to see Clint Eastwood in *The Outlaw Josey Wales*, a clip from the trailer fixed in permanent memory, the moment when a bounty hunter tracking Eastwood muttered to his partner: 'Not a hard man to follow. Leaves bodies everywhere.' Brian adored this remark, and used to repeat it under his breath at moments of stress during the day, to beneficial effect. He could not now recall where he had heard about a revival screening at the British Film Institute down on the South Bank, just when he had given up hope of ever seeing the movie. Grateful for such a good thing happening to him, by chance, unexpected, unearned, Brian bought himself a ticket.

It was excellent, not in the least bit disappointing, stuffed with tenderness and vengeance. Eastwood, who directed as well as starred, spent much of the film in the saddle and for this feat of skill and endurance promptly became Brian's movie idol. For other reasons too: the lyricism of the Texan landscape through which Josey Wales pursued without mercy the Unionist guerrillas, killers of his wife and children; and for the depiction of peasant farmers of Missouri as people with hopes and pain.

This was only the second time Brian had been to the

BFI, twenty years after his first visit, when he was nineteen, taken to see *Kes* along with two other youngsters by the manager at their hostel, to show them, Mr Trevor had said, that positive things do sometimes turn up, replacing hardship. Or something like that. It felt long ago, a period from which Brian had managed to move on, without ever finding a comfortable alternative place for himself.

Throughout the early years of his working life Brian had tried as best he could to participate, handicapped by never knowing what to say to anyone. Within a group of people he felt pushed to the periphery, quickly aware that nobody much minded whether he turned up or not. He had joined a book-reading club, mostly of women, jolly, middle-aged, who ridiculed his proposals of novels to read, listened in silence to his halting comments on the book-of-the-month and moved promptly on to topics of their own concern. In another attempt at company, he took up football. Not playing, of course, he was hopeless at sport, but watching, becoming a home supporter at West Ham. This was a failure too, leaving him post-match on Saturday evenings with an even greater sense of isolation. At the time he had liked the idea of being part of a loyal crowd and it was the individual men nearby on the terraces who troubled him, their spray of shouted abuse at the opposition, the tribal jokes and gang laughter. He longed to be included, and dreaded it, equally. During these interim years he had had various jobs and an assortment of rented rooms. His first place in London was the one he had liked best, the dormitory in the St Pancras hostel where he had stayed for years, until Mr Trevor felt obliged to turf him out for being far beyond the age limit. He had eventually ended up alone in his present small rented flat above the Taj Mahal on Kentish Town Road, which he found perfectly adequate.

In the process of settling into his new home Brian had taken four long walks from the front door, north, south, east and west, needing the security of a physical sense of where he lived. At home on dark winter evenings after work he wanted, for safety's sake, accurately to picture in his head the streets and houses and shops around him. It was on one of these exploratory tours that he had come across Talacre Gardens, after which he regularly took the short walk down Prince of Wales Road for a constitutional twice round the perimeter of the park and, in the summer, to sit and read on a bench. The seat he liked best, in the shade of a horse chestnut tree, was near one of the playgrounds, surrounded by a low wire fence over which balls and balloons escaped and which Brian used to retrieve and throw back. Two boys, brothers Brian guessed from their matching clothes and blond hair, invented the ritual game of deliberately tossing the balls out again, urging Brian to trot across the grass to pick them up and throw them back inside.

There was lots of laughter, from Brian too.

Walking slowly home, Brian thought of his own brother, Peter, nine years his senior, with whom he was unable to remember ever laughing. They barely knew each other, had never lived in the same house. Brian stopped suddenly in the street, muttering to himself, and stamped on the pavement several times one foot after the other, furious that playing with those two nice boys had awakened images of Peter and his father and their treatment of his mother.

With an effort he managed to clear his head of unwanted family memories and continued on into Kentish Town Road.

At Talacre one weekend a woman had walked over to Brian's bench and introduced herself as Dorothy,

Camden Council's manager of the playground. She had noticed the gentle way he had been playing with the children on and off all summer and, being short of staff at weekends, she wondered if he might agree to keep volunteer-watch over the facility for a fixed couple of hours on Sunday mornings. The thought of community participation, of acceptance within a worthwhile group of local people delighted Brian and when, as it always seemed to, everything fell apart he felt especially hurt. Two mothers had complained about his unqualified status and, with regret, Dorothy asked him not to come again. For his own sake it might be safest if he did not visit the gardens at all for the time being, Dorothy warned, as his accusers were a vindictive pair.

Brian's instinctive act of self-protection was to narrow his free time down to film.

For several years he had promised himself he would become a member at the British Film Institute, failing to do so for no reason other than the trepidation he generally felt about doing anything new. The Talacre Gardens fiasco impelled urgent action and after a visit to the watch-repairer in The Cut on a Saturday afternoon not long after seeing *The Outlaw Josey Wales,* Brian grasped the moment, walked on over to the South Bank and filled in the inexpensive BFI membership form. He felt a rush of rightness as he placed a copy of the month's programme in his bag to study at home. From then on, he booked in for a screening at least every couple of weeks, berating himself for not having done so sooner.

Why ever not, he wondered. Why had he delayed till he was almost forty to do something so obviously right for him?

Not laziness; he had never been lazy not even as a boy, taking himself off on numberless bicycle rides up and down and around the streets of Magheramorne, to keep out of the way, a strategy terminated by escape to England with his mother. The difficulty, that to a certain extent he had always faced and which grew worse with age, was his dwelling on the multiple possible consequences of a single act and feeling the need to precision-weigh the varied benefits and costs. This took time to work out, sometimes a long time, so long that, by the end of the process, circumstances had often changed and the whole palaver of assessment had to begin all over again. Membership of the British Film Institute was not to be undertaken lightly, Brian felt, sensing that it raised the watching of film to a new level of commitment and responsibility. The dilemmas had repeated themselves with variations night after night as Brian lay in bed above the Taj Mahal wondering what the right thing to do was, questioning his ability to treat film with the seriousness it deserved.

Which was why, Brian concluded, dwelling also on his past failures to feel accepted, it had taken an age to become a member.

He mentioned the idea of making film his thing to Lorenzo at Il Castelletto, the café off Camden High Street where he had lunch every day of the week – at 2.15 p.m., to avoid the crush. With his brother Dario the third generation of Cerolis to run the café, Lorenzo went to music gigs in any spare time from the myriad family obligations of the Italian clan where he lived in East London. Friends of his had put together an irregular band in which he occasionally played guitar, its case poking out from behind the counter, stacked with the hot water boiler for tea, pampered espresso coffee machine and a rainbow assortment of mugs. Over the years Brian had come to trust Lorenzo, moved by his kindness to the customers for whom Il Castelletto was a refuge, perhaps the only

13

public place in their day where they felt safe and wanted. Regulars like Marian, a neatly dressed middle-aged
secretary at the gasworks, who came in twice each day,
for an early coffee and late lunch, and was sometimes
obliged to share Brian's table by the door. At such times
he witnessed close up the release of tension in her face at
Lorenzo's welcome and, from his own isolation, guessed
that the hand placed on her shoulder and pantomime
flattery amounted to Marian's major human contact of
the day. However busy with serving and clearing other
tables, Lorenzo listened attentively to her home decorat-
ing preoccupations, responding with DIY stories of his
own in Bow. Marian asked to borrow an unfinished pot of
the paint he had chosen for his kitchen, to try out in hers.

No problem, he said.

Nothing was a problem to Lorenzo in his mission to
please.

One quiet afternoon, on finishing his lunch of cot-
tage pie and vegetables followed by apple crumble with
custard, Brian peripherally broached the subject of his
current concerns, the increasing dominance of film in his
life, asking Lorenzo how he managed to prevent his love
of indie rock from taking over.

How did he keep things in proportion, Brian wondered.

My kids, Lorenzo replied. They need me more than I
need my guitar.

Oh!

Brian was taken aback. He never pictured Lorenzo
married, with children, although he knew perfectly well
that he was.

He found himself trying to explain how, living alone,
it was possible for him to let things get out of hand. Out
of proportion. Like forgetting to anticipate where the exit
was on the Kentish Town platform and walking in the

wrong direction at Waterloo so that he sat in the opposite end of the tube, having to walk its length again once he alighted. It did not matter at all. And yet it did. To Brian it felt a disgraceful failure of judgement.

Give yourself a break, Brian. You're a decent bloke. Treat yourself better, Lorenzo said, giving him a soft pat on the shoulder. Must get on. See you tomorrow.

Without deciding to do so, indeed without really noticing the change, Brian's BFI visits multiplied over the initial months of membership from once a fortnight to once a week, to twice on weekdays and once each weekend. To step up another notch and become a nightly regular like the select band of dedicated BFI buffs was a conscious decision, mulled over, wrestled with and yes-and-no-ed numerous times. Brian was aware of two things, principally, that finally impelled him into this life-altering commitment. One was the dark feelings that had begun to envelop him on his nights alone at home, where he had stopped bothering to make himself hot food and too often was unable to remember a single thing from the hours of television he sat slumped in front of, incapable of participation the next day at coffee-break chat in the office about the night's viewing. He had also stopped reading, which was a more serious worry, and eczema had erupted on his elbows and behind his knees. At work he managed to present a brave face, nobody seeming to notice his despair. If they did, they said nothing. Nor would he have expected them to, avoidance of the personal an unwritten office rule. Brian kept himself to himself and did not know anyone well enough – or want to – for a proper conversation. He recognized the danger of disintegration and that he needed release somehow from the pressure in his head. Film, he reckoned, might be the answer.

Looked at from a positive perspective, Brian's main reason for thinking of becoming an every-night regular at the British Film Institute was the regulars themselves: the disparate group of middle-aged men, six or seven most nights, whom he had observed with envy in their self-absorbed discussions in an isolated corner of the foyer. The more he saw of them, edging close enough on occasion to eavesdrop, the deeper his desire to take part.

Being the kind of person who needed a sheaf of reasons to act, Brian numbered off in his notebook a list of the other affirmative points: the prospect of repeated free visits to the newly opened Museum of the Moving Image at the back of the BFI; big reduction in heating bills by spending his evenings away from home; the satisfaction of mapping out a monthly schedule, marking the titles and times in his diary and relaxing in the knowledge that everything was arranged, any threat of surprise minimized; and, permeating all aspects of his imagined new life, the infinite delight of film.

Brian became a nightly regular.

The first film he saw at the BFI in his new capacity was a preview screening of *The Fruit Machine*, the fictional name of a gay nightclub in Brighton, with Annabelle – a.k.a. the comedian Robbie Coltrane – as mistress of ceremonies. Brian had enjoyed the year before Coltrane's TV portrayal of Samuel Johnson in *Blackadder the Third*, and memory of this pleasure fed into his disappointment in the movie's confusing shenanigans, the transvestite murder at the seaside neither funny nor especially tragic.

Never mind. There were some good things in it, as in every film, he told himself.

Rehearsing remarks for his role of buff-in-the-making, Brian noted the similarities between Eddie in *The Fruit Machine* and Johnny in *My Beautiful Laundrette* of three years earlier, both with blond streak on top, cap on the back of the head, similar age and same sexual leaning. Different skin colour, but that did not matter.

Participation in the gathering of buffs appeared to be unconditional – the fact that they were all white males, no women, was more a matter of endemic social habit than the individual prejudice of the buffs, Brian felt, in recognition of his own narrow conventions. Drawing on maximum courage a couple of evenings after his switch to movie-a-night, Brian sidled up to the small group of men standing close together in a corner of the NFT 1 foyer and joined the circle. No cold shoulder. No sudden silence. He smiled nervously in a general way at the group, two of whom smiled back an easy-going welcome. Nobody asked him his name or anything about his job, the conversation exclusively about film, to Brian's relief. As none of them appeared to address anybody by name there was no false familiarity, no banality, no banter, no point-scoring, and in those early days Brian felt received with greater warmth by almost all of the shifting band of regulars at the BFI than he had ever experienced anywhere else in his entire life.

The joy went to Brian's head and during his second week as a regular he said much too much both before and after the screenings, spoke too quickly, too loudly, his voice rising in excitement to a cartoon squeak. The height of Brian's new-boy excess emerged after a first-run showing of *Bird*, with Forest Whitaker as Charlie Yardbird Parker, directed and produced by Clint Eastwood. Brian's intemperate behaviour was explained, though not excused, by the fact that he had recently read a second-hand copy of *Bird Lives!*, the music journalist Ross Russell's biography of the saxophonist. In a muddle of emotion, Brian tried to summarize all at once this detailed, committed book, to relate it to the film, and to praise Eastwood's direction. Aware of failing to make significant sense, Brian talked faster and faster until forced to stop and draw breath. During the pause he was shocked when one of the regulars pointed out something he had neglected to observe, that Whitaker looked uncannily similar to Parker at his zenith, to the extent of moving with the instrument in performance like a bebop revolutionary, despite never before having played the saxophone.

Whitaker's own son Damon portrayed Parker as a boy, sealing the familial likeness, someone else added, when Brian had been shamed into silence.

On the night after the *Bird* debacle Brian held his nerve, resisting the temptation to turn tail, and took the risk of turning up at the BFI. To his surprise he was treated no differently, for safety's sake nevertheless preserving a benign silence for the remainder of the week.

Separate from their gang was a small group of occasional moviegoers, women as well as men, whose presence Brian was conscious of from time to time. One of them, he noticed when the man stood in front of him in the queue waiting for delayed entry to NFT 2, smelt heavily of perfumed deodorant. Though Brian was confident his own body odour was under control, he could not deny catching a stale whiff of sweat from one or two of his lot. Daring to take a good look one evening at the rival set, he was astonished to notice that they talked to each other very differently from the way he and his friends did, with greater intimacy, even physical contact.

Friends?

None of the buffs were his friends, Brian admitted, keen to accept the truth when he saw it. Not that it mattered, but he assumed they were unmarried and suspected that, like him, they mostly lived alone.

18

There was one man whom he hoped might become a friend, but as yet he was simply a fellow regular. Something the man had said one night felt revelatory: that truth was not a crystal to be stored in a drawer but a fluid into which one falls head first. Brian had never before come across such ways of thinking.

Maybe the rival group, fewer in number and sporadic in their attendance, were in fact ordinary friends on arranged evenings out together? Chatting as-often-as-not of non-film things, such as the Lockerbie disaster which at Christmas Brian had overheard them discussing at length.

Another of life's mysteries.

There were times when Brian felt that the only thing he understood anything about was film.

Nothing much else made sense.

Not that he could always make sense of the movies he saw either, straight understanding not the point in film. Take Ingmar Bergman, one of the BFI programmers' favourites, a bias of which Brian approved, attending most screenings of the Swede's films, especially impressed by *The Seventh Seal* and *Persona*, though neither of these films could he rationally explain from beginning to end. This did not stop him adoring Bergman's women. Not sexually, the idea of any woman as an object of his physical desire Brian had barred from consciousness. No, he cherished Bibi Andersson as a person, for her utterly alive presence on screen, her tenderness and laughter, the actor who played the nurse in *Persona* who above everything else was the personification of womanhood. Brian used to believe that Bergman could never make a film that he would not like – until seeing the maestro's most recent movie, *Fanny and Alexander*.

That really was a dud, the director's seductive stack of

wives and lovers sadly absent from the screen, Brian had commented at their post-screening discussion.

Bergman's last movie?

Possibly, an old man now, tired and recalcitrant.

In his daily life Brian was endlessly anxious, often about the same repeated, insignificant and ridiculous things. Knowing his worries were nonsensical made little difference, he still panicked, returning to the flat when about to board the bus, to check that the window of his bedroom was closed, more distressed by the idea of maybe having made a mistake than by the unlikely danger of a break-in, with nothing of value to steal. Brian physically anticipated in advance the trajectories of each day, picturing himself walking ahead to a particular bus stop, holding out an arm and getting on, getting off and turning left in his mind, second right, then left again. Methodically he ticked off the details, the weather in his mental map mild, grey, featureless, helping him achieve the illusion of dull composure. The duller the better. No change meant no challenge, steady ahead.

Except in the worst of circumstances, Brian was sufficiently self-aware to know that it was he who generated the feelings of helplessness, not something or somebody outside. All the same, he accepted no excuse for error, allowed no means of recovery or forgiveness. The only method he could think of to soften his fears was this pre-imagining of the day's chores. What time to take his trousers to the Camden Town dry cleaners, then when to collect them, finding conflicting reasons to waver back and forth, paralyzed by the simplest of decisions. There were mornings slumped in a seat on the tube on the way to work when Brian repeated over and over in his head the words he planned to say to Mr Wilson, his section manager, nothing of great importance, maybe a marginal shift of filing method, about which he managed to work himself into a state of insane unease.

He was afraid of saying the wrong thing, of having failed to learn from some earlier error which had slipped his mind.

Learn quick as lightning from your mistakes or die, his mother melodramatically threatened him as a boy. And meant it, he had come to understand.

Ingrained expectations of disaster cushioned Brian against the potential trauma of the most challenging of the films he saw during his first months as a novice buff, notably *Burning Angel*, made in Finland from a true-life incident, the suicide of a psychiatric nurse. A successful young model from Helsinki played the lead, in her first film, a performance of gauche beauty which mesmerized Brian. Her vulnerability touched his own, forcing him to push down inside against the swell of locked memories. Afterwards he read with caution the detailed programme note supplied each night by the BFI, primed to turn aside if the text approached too close, and was moved by the remarks of the Finnish director, a woman, quoted by the BFI curator:

> This is not a 'message film'. It simply sets out to tell a story about a topic that touches all of us. I wanted to show that a young person's mind can suffer terrible upsets, that ghastly things occur in life, but they may change subsequently into valuable building blocks for one's later life.

Hope in adversity, as Brian put it to himself.

Tuned to failure, Brian was poorly prepared for the better things which came his way from time to time. One such thing took place during his fourth week as a regular, which sealed his fate and propelled him into unquestioning commitment to seven nights a week at the BFI.

Distant Voices, Still Lives, set in Liverpool and based on the director Terence Davies's boyhood, was in effect two short films made into one of standard length, *Still Lives* not started until two years after *Distant Voices* was completed. The break, due to lack of funds, was marked by a lift of mood in the director's narrative voice, released by the death of his tyrannical father – played by an actor Brian admired, Pete Postlethwaite. Davies told the audience at the Q & A after the screening: 'I said to my mother, why did you not just kill him? If it had been me, and this is true, I would have waited until he was asleep and I would have put a pillow over his face. But she was not like me.'

Brian made the vital discovery that night that something he needed to be true proved to be so: that a nakedly emotional film on themes and feelings close to his own story did not necessarily shake alive his stifled memories of the past.

He was safe. The narratives of others were not his. Able without too much trouble to resist identifying with Davies's film, in a burst of relief Brian felt ready to watch anything the BFI chose to show.

He was not unmoved.

Far from it.

The wedding scene was amazing, with the bad-tempered groom overwhelmed by his new bride's eight sisters and effeminate little brother, a child actor playing Davies, the youngest sibling.

The importance of religion in Davies's altar-boy upbringing mirrored Brian's, in reverse, a bonny Catholic and bigoted Prot, adolescent scouser versus nascent Orangeman. The church's condemnation of gays was one of many issues which had made Davies into a devout atheist, the director told the audience, a remark applauded by Brian in his own adult certainty that man created God rather than the other way round.

You'd think we could have made a better job of putting together imaginary figureheads, Brian added to himself. And avoided centuries of murderous mayhem in religion's competing names.

If anything, Brian was a bit of a Buddhist, he reckoned, in honour of his interest in Japan, one of the few distant parts of the world he knew anything about.

As Brian did not yet feel wholly comfortable at the buffs' gatherings after his loss of dignity with the Charlie Parker film, to preserve his post-event sense of well-being after the moving experience of *Distant Voices, Still Lives*, he slipped out of the back entrance to walk fast in the rain up to catch the Northern Line at Waterloo Station. The train to High Barnet via Kentish Town when it finally arrived was more crowded than usual, because of the weather, and Brian's attention was caught by the wounded face of a middle-aged woman across the aisle wearing a shapeless coat and see-through plastic hood, a latter-day version, he decided, of Terence Davies's mother in the film. On arrival home he switched on the electric fire, boiled the kettle and settled down with his mug of tea to read the BFI programme notes, kept till after the screening, wishing to watch films free of critical influence and make up his own mind. When the small room had warmed up sufficiently, he removed his coat and hung it on a hook on the back of the door. Later he ran a hot bath, as he did every evening from his trusted Combi boiler, this single physical treat of a normal day sending him to cautious sleep, curled on his side in his short single bed.

He was not tall, and slept in a ball, able to avoid the fuss of replacing the bed he had acquired with the flat.

Before closing his eyes Brian thought about the screening earlier in the week of another newly seen film, set in Dublin, *The Lonely Passion of Judith Hearne*, of which George Harrison was the executive producer, in his post-Beatles identity. Before being able to relax Brian needed to silence the Irish echoes from a film doused in drunkenness, pious sanctimony and stubborn self-destruction.

Brian had lived in Kent as a boy, Kentish Town as a man and valued the irrational sense of continuity from their matching names. He had found his flat on the Kentish Town Road a few months after securing his post in the Camden Housing Department, a definite step up from his clerk's job at a large builder's merchant in Clapham, where he had occupied for a time a basement bedsit opposite the Royal Mail Parcels Office, disturbed by the night-time comings and goings of lorries and vans. In his quiet way Brian felt blessed by the move from Clapham to Camden, from South to North London. The street door to Brian's flat opened to a narrow passage leading towards a single flight of stairs, his sitting room window looking out over the flat bitumen roof of the restaurant, onto which the wind had blown varied debris. His perfunctory lease, in practice renewable yearly for as long as he wished, included furniture and fittings, much of which he gave to the house clearance people when they delivered the simple desk, a long ceiling-high storage and bookcase unit, and the small kitchen table and chairs he had purchased from them. Brian kept his possessions to a minimum, nothing left lying around, everything put safely back in its appointed place on completion of use. It had taken him an entire weekend to scrub and dust the flat before he felt able to move in, after which he kept his home decently clean. The bathroom was bigger than the kitchen, which suited him fine. He did not care about the colour of the walls and had never bothered to decorate.

During all his time in the employment of Camden Council, Brian had worked in the rates section, recently promoted to be the sole member of staff responsible for keeping up to date the lease and freehold records, a task he fulfilled with the efficiency of an experienced book-keeper. In the office, as everywhere else, Brian did his best not to be noticed. He was neatly dressed, his jackets in various shades of dark blue, with grey trousers, usually a white shirt and inoffensive tie, on time to arrive and to leave, seldom spending a minute longer at his desk than stipulated in his terms of employment. At non-working weekends he wore the same clothes, occasionally dis-carding the tie in the summer.

Record keeping in the Housing Office had moved away from the leather-bound ledgers of post-war vin-tage to a large cross-referenced card index of ownership, in essence Brian's invention, built on the system he had devised for stock movements in and out of the ex-tensive builder's yard off Clapham Common where he had worked previously. The cards came in five primary colours and were themselves then colour-coded with six different tinted tapes on the marker lobes. The informa-tion was delivered to a rack of wire baskets on Brian's desk from various sources, internal and external, and he altered the cards accordingly, the work which piled up in his in-trays sometimes taking him days to empty. At other times, with the backlog cleared, he occupied himself double-checking the files, correcting and perfecting his system of codes. He liked the static responsibilities of his job and put up with the elements of office life he objected to. Such as the hullabaloo of the annual sweepstake on the Grand National, and the custom of birthday bumps, executed on the clear space of carpet outside the lift. They threatened to award Brian an official birthday if he continued to refuse to tell them the actual date. When he turned even paler and stiffer than usual at this threat they moved on to a more entertaining victim.

With the vague aim of righting a long-past wrong, Brian became involved with the interdepartmental Camden Council Choral Society, an unlikely outfit sustained by the enthusiasm of one of the borough's in-house solicitors. They met once a month to rehearse for an annual public performance at the Roundhouse, up the road in Chalk Farm, after which the councillors held a staff party. This year's work, short and difficult, was Allegri's *Miserere*, two choirs of four and of five voices singing in polyphony, amongst which the twenty or so members of the CCCS were spread, voices doubled, even tripled in this messy adaption. Brian was a tenor, his perceptive ear compensating for an inability to read music. As a boy of eight, within days of her release from prison his mother had collected Brian from the children's home in Magheramorne and taken him with her over the water and down to Rochester in Kent, committed to continuing from there her work with the Ulster Volunteer Force. In need of help with her slow, lonely little boy, she had hitched up with the local Presbyterians and enrolled him in their small church choir. Which he detested, for a host of reasons. Bullied from the start by the other choristers, for his accent and feeble physique, and for his refusal to participate in the boys' escapades, Brian had needed a way out. He found it by convincing his mother and the minister that he was tone-deaf, thus removing himself from church activities.

From an early age he had mostly been pretty good

at refusing to do the things he disliked. Thin, shy, and sandy-haired as a boy, Brian was better self-protected than he looked.

Working out what he did like had turned out to be more of a challenge than dealing with the dangers. Much more. Exacerbated by his habitual hesitancy at saying yes to anything.

Saying no, on the other hand, remained a lifelong ability, leading to his implacable withdrawal from the Camden Council Choral Society two weeks before their Roundhouse concert. Oblivious to the conductor's complaints and to Mr Wilson's disappointment, he resigned from the choir as soon as he had proved to his own satisfaction that he could sing in tune. The close proximity at rehearsal of human bodies had become upsetting and, with relief, he reverted while at work to single-minded focus on the Council's register of property ownership, armed with this additional evidence, if proof were needed, that he would never be a team player.

As far as Brian was concerned, he was destined to remain bent over his housing department desk until retirement, his practice of steady independence sharpened to the point where there was nothing much he needed to say to any of his colleagues day-by-day. With his soft coastal-Kent voice and rubber soled shoes he had become semi-transparent, a spectral figure in his unchangingly neat corner of the scruffy open-plan office.

By now his separateness was by personal choice, he felt, not through the imposition of others. Turning away from the social round at work and living alone, never inviting anybody home to the flat, inevitably resulted in his exclusion from everyday togetherness. Which was for the best, he told himself. People scared him, especially the crush and crescendo of after-office pubs. A secret teetotaller, he pretended to drink, dipping his lips into a half-pint of beer and hiding his still-full glass behind the ice-bucket on the bar when he soon left. His office lot, the women as much as the men, liked nothing better than to storm about the place in gangs. Peals of loud laughter rang out and miniature bottles of vodka appeared from purses on outings to West End shows, weekend trips to Brighton, late night tenpin bowling off the North Circular Road – feeling fully themselves only in the company of others.

Brian was the opposite, barely able to recognize himself unless alone.

He did not go on any of these outings, was never invited, and disliked having to listen over the following week to the increasingly exaggerated reminiscences.

On his grimmest days in the office Brian skipped lunch at Lorenzo's and hurried down the road to the Odeon, dropping into the darkness at the back of the cinema in the middle of whatever happened to be showing. He always had to leave to return to work before the end, but did not mind, refreshed by a dose of film. Mystified one lunchtime as to why clever Anthony Hopkins was behind bars in *The Silence of the Lambs*, he had returned to the Odeon the next Saturday afternoon to see the whole film, and was shocked by the manipulative deceit of the Hopkins character, serial killer and cannibal Dr Hannibal Lecter.

In his excitement at acceptance by the buffs at the BFI, Brian made the mistake of telling someone in the office of his devotion to film, and the colleague informed others. Unable one morning to escape a coffee trolley chat about the movies with his boss, Mr Wilson, Brian umm-ed and err-ed his way through an unwilling conversation. Asked what his favourite kind of film was, he was unable to utter

28

a single syllable in reply and stood rigid, jaw locked, staring across the room – until a conversation-halting answer sprang to mind.

Kon Ichikawa's kabuki scenes.

His boss did say one interesting thing as he multi-sugared his coffee, about what he imagined to be the pleasure of losing oneself in going often to the cinema, the joy of immersion, he suggested, like diving into the warm sea on holiday in Malta. There was a time when this, more-or-less, was Brian's view too, before he became a BFI regular, when it dawned on him that the opposite was true, that being a buff was the consummation of self, that at work or on the tube and in those dreadful sessions in the pub he was not himself at all, was no-one, nothing, in fact, and it was only in the cinema that he became a person.

Brian said none of this to Mr Wilson. In retrospect he felt a bit guilty at his kabuki putdown, by referring to elements of the only Ichikawa film he had so far seen, the brilliantly beautiful *An Actor's Revenge*.

Great name, Kon Ichikawa.

Brian was longing to see more of the director's movies.

It was in pursuit of another of his Japanese director heroes, Nagisa Oshima, that Brian ventured one weekend into foreign territory, the multi-million Butler's Wharf development on the south side of Tower Bridge. Earlier in the decade Oshima had made a film with David Bowie, props and ephemera from which were included in the exhibition *Inventing Ziggy Stardust* at the new Design Museum on Shad Thames, keyed to the relationships between the singer and his artist collaborators in concert, publication, and film. Emerging from Tower Hill Underground Brian found himself in an unfamiliar London landscape, which felt as if he was walking through abandoned lots in a giant film studio, past the location of his favourite slasher movie, then across Tower Bridge, an emblematic presence in *The Long Good Friday*, and over to the far side of the river and a set straight from *Blade Runner*, a narrow alley between tall warehouses below walkways running at different heights and angles between the buildings, the air heavy with the stench of slaughtered fish. True to futuristic film tradition, the journey ended with Bowie, a creature from the beyond, earthbound in the modernist white spaceship of the Design Museum tethered on the banks of the Thames.

Brian had yet to see a screening of Oshima's *Merry Christmas Mr. Lawrence*, filmed in the conventional setting of a Japanese prisoner of war camp, with Bowie as Maj. Jack 'Strafer' Celliers and Tom Conti as Lt. Col. John Lawrence, these two the main British actors in the movie. A fellow buff whose judgement Brian trusted, an expert on film music, had warned him not to rush to see this particular Oshima, which was over stylized, in his view, and suffered from a turgid Sakamoto score, its un-Japanese title taken from the final spoken words of the film. To be in the presence of actual film props was new to Brian, an experience which – despite the cautionary advice – imparted a palpable sense of connectedness to the practice of filmmaking. He stared at length into the glass case containing the camp commander Captain Yonoi's military baton and samurai sword, beside a honey-coloured lock of Bowie's hair, supposedly cut from his head while buried vertically up to his neck in sand. A mint *Merry Christmas Mr. Lawrence* poster from the Cannes Film Festival was hanging on the stairs and bore the quote 'inside each heart another battle raged' – no help to Brian's understanding of what the film might essentially be about. On display in an adjacent cabinet, he inspected

30

material from a Bowie film he knew and liked, the shiny gun and chain from *The Man Who Fell to Earth* directed by Nicolas Roeg, a pair of tinted spectacles seen in several different photo portraits of the Thin White Duke, and the sweater and scarf worn for his screen introduction to a children's favourite, *The Snowman*. The main focus of the exhibition was the design of Bowie record covers, a field with which Brian was unfamiliar, the musical phenomenon of Major Tom having largely passed him by. All the same, he liked the images he saw and would have stayed longer had not a noisy group of art students and their tutor arrived to disrupt his concentration.

Unease in everyday crowds affected Brian's moviegoing, making the BFI his natural home, where even on the night of a full-house there was no pushing or shoving, no popcorn. Some whistles and cheers at premieres, that was all, Brian himself joining in on occasion. Paranoid about control, he took steps to avoid any suggestion of being part of a popular pack, wary of box office movies praised in the press which he preferred to see on repeat scheduling a year or two later, by which time the hype had subsided and he could watch them with his own eyes. Although Brian was frequently unaware of the precise reasons why he behaved as he did, he broadly knew that vulnerability was involved and that he needed to be careful not to put himself under too much pressure. Becoming a nightly film buff tied him down to the safety of repetition.

Brian returned to fully active participation in the regulars' discussions following the London preview of Jean-Claude Sussfeld's *The Catwalk*, pointing out at their after-film chat a comment on the information sheet about 'overdone buff quotations' in which a newspaper reviewer had cited specific thefts by Sussfeld from Kubrick in *The Shining* and Hitchcock in *Rear Window*. The buffs laughed in recognition of their own foibles and proceeded to pool the humorous plagiarisms they too had noticed. Brian felt exonerated, able to forgive himself for the earlier lapse, happy to sense his acceptance. There were times when it seemed to him that everyone else his age was an adult, whereas he was a child in disguise.

He always found something of interest to pick up at gatherings of the regulars. After the BFI interview with Karel Reisz for the preview screening of his film *Everybody Wins*, a well-connected buff revealed that in the company of his uncle, a theatrical agent, he once had tea with Reisz and his American actress wife Betsy Blair at their home in Chalcot Gardens, off Haverstock Hill.

No! What was it like? Brian asked, incredulously.

The house or director? Laugh a minute. Can't remember the details, regrettably. I was only six at the time.

Brian had already made a note in his diary of Reisz's remark in the on-stage conversation:

> In *Everybody Wins* I found discovering the realities of small-town life through the distorting prism of an appealing, seductive, but fear-ridden woman very compelling.

A quote destined for Brian's growing store of notes on directing sexual provocation in film. His immediate previous entry was from an interview with Myriam Mézières, co-star of Alain Tanner's *A Flame in my Heart*:

> There's a gap in the cinema between sex scenes done with good taste and those done with the cold naturalism you find in porno movies. I wanted to see if, for once in my life, I could show something different on screen. I can't really put a name to it, which is what makes it so exciting. Love scenes with joy – and by that I don't mean

exhibitionism. More the opposite. I'm rather shy in real life but when I'm on set or in front of the camera slip into another skin. It may be obvious to say that but it's true.

At the eighth London Lesbian and Gay Film Festival the other day Brian was impressed by *Belle*, the directorial debut of Dutch writer and singer Irma Achten, whose future work he took note to look out for. Her thoughtful commitment contrasted with the bluster of two billboard males whose films Brian had also recently seen, Klaus Kinski's *Paganini* and Dennis Hopper's *Catchfire*, the latter moonlighting as Alan Smithee to direct while retaining his own name to star in the role of Milo, a professional killer and obsessive.

Maybe he knew he was a better actor than director, Brian conjectured.

Any good as a photographer? one of the regulars enquired.

Standard fashionable shots, intervened the tall buff in heavy-rimmed glasses. Divorce junkie, Hopper. Another film star who needs to be loved, and never is. Once a woman gets up close.

Good at loving himself, someone else added, unusually one of eight regulars at that particular screening.

Prompting Brian to think of Kinski's insane vanity, so much so, he reckoned, that the German's performances on screen were capable of inhabiting a unique world of anguished exaggeration and, as such, could be extraordinary.

In Werner Herzog's *Aguirre, The Wrath of God*, for instance, the jewel of a film.

Without the firm hand of Herzog, Kinski directing himself in *Paganini* was a disaster. To the extent that Brian found the film actively offensive, spattered with gratuitous sex, pseudo-Satanism and a tragically bad cameo performance by Marcel Marceau, once the master of mime. Kinski had died earlier in the month in which Brian had seen *Paganini* at the BFI, of a heart attack in California, within two years of making this dismal last film.

The regulars were inclined to watch more classic cinema than contemporary, on various elements of which individual buffs had made themselves expert. Although he had not yet seen as much as he would like to, Brian had developed a keen affinity with Japanese film of the post-war period and was excited to find that the BFI had programmed *Early Spring*, made in 1956 by the master, Yasujirō Ozu.

Brian prided himself on seldom taking films personally, pleased to concentrate instead on what appeared to matter to the people making them, to the cinematographer and sound designer as well as director and producer. To his surprise – for the narrative was slow, generous, with no dramatic denouement – *Early Spring* proved to be one of the exceptions, triggering inner identification. Nothing much happened, other than the repeated trek by commuter train to and from work in the city and a drunken party or two after office hours, plus the traditional wake following a colleague's decease. Nothingness was the point of this finely judged film, as visible in the scene which touched Brian closest, taking place in a small Tokyo tavern where a grey-haired man was perched leaning over the wooden bar, halfway drunk yet sober enough to talk succinctly about his imminent retirement after thirty-one years working for the same company. The barman spoke out optimistically in an attempt to lighten his customer's mood, suggesting how proud he must be of his solid service, looking forward now to a life of leisure with a good pension. Not at all, the man corrected, after tax and the expense of moving, there would be nothing much left. For years as a good company man, he had dreamed of one day opening a bookshop, near a school, quietly serving the young and their mothers. He could not now afford to, assuring the barman that there was nothing left in retirement for company men like him but boredom and death.

Conscious of the value of brevity, Brian reserved his remarks on *Early Spring* to fellow regulars to a single comment, on the expressive use of the fan by Ozu's women, silent words darting across the tatami at the altered flutter of a hand.

Wonderfully restrained percussive score, Brian added, to himself.

Marimba, he reckoned, having read some time ago an English-language book on Japanese music and listened repeatedly to the virtuoso performer Keiko Abe, a tape of whose he owned, entranced by the percussive sounds she made.

Japanese cinema was a subject sufficiently obscure to Londoners for Brian to feel safe in seeking to make it his own.

Given the day-by-day anxieties with which Brian contended, the ability to focus attention on the niceties of film was effective distraction from an existence beset on the outside by recurring banalities. In his late twenties Brian had become chronically constipated and it was only when he rented alone his flat on Kentish Town Road and could relax in his own bathroom that his bowel movements resumed a relatively normal pattern. Treasuring the change, he adopted the habit of shitting only at home, saving himself the gut-clenching embarrassment he felt with someone else in the next-door public cubicle, hearing them and – worse still – himself being heard.

A veteran of concealment and evasion, Brian was none-theless unable to control his mounting sighs of strain on the lavatory, before a half-stifled cry of rectal release. On those occasions when he could not hold out till returning home, he went to the basement Gents at the BFI and stayed seated on the toilet after he had finished until extra-sure that the man next door had flushed and departed. Then he unlocked his door, dashed his hands under the basin tap and hurriedly left, without risking the time to dry them. Not knowing what others in the cubicles looked like, the disaster of recognition was averted.

On film it was different.

Everything was.

One of Brian's favourite film moments – from a cast of dozens, admittedly – was in Wim Wenders's *Kings of the Road*, the scene where a vehicle drew up in a deserted landscape somewhere near the East German border and Rüdiger Vogler walked off twenty yards from the road to take a shit. The camera focused low down to film from behind a long dark sausage turd drop slowly from a pale arse.

In black and white.

Brian admired the shot and always wondered if it was Vogler's bum or a stunt man's.

At what time of day was it filmed?

How many inadequate excretions preceded this perfect take?

Cinema raised more questions in his mind than could ever be answered.

Brian used to imagine that Wenders's early films were made the same way that he himself sometimes opened his eyes on waking and just looked, not trying to prove or understand anything.

Although there were multiple examples of men

pissing on film, none of them commanded a special place in Brian's memory like *Kings of the Road*. Nor did he harbour anxiety about himself peeing in public. At the BFI's urinals he held his cock in one hand and casually shielded it from prying sight with the other.

Out of modesty.

Not that there was anything down there to write home about, as far as he was aware.

Once Brian's film rota had settled into place, things continued in steady rhythm year after year, made affordable by ticket-price reductions for registered regulars and a relatively short, inexpensive distance to travel.

He felt fortunate in having alternative routes direct from cinema to home, either by tube on the Northern Line from both Waterloo and Embankment to Kentish Town, or the 168 bus from Waterloo Bridge to a stop on the Kentish Town Road fifty yards from his flat. With a resident's travelcard he was at liberty to take either, on whim. The few changes in his routine – refinements, he called them – developed without fuss.

With the basic structure of life in position there were always little things new and old which needed sorting out. Brian was uncertain, for instance, whether not-eating in the BFI's cinemas was the actual rule or an unwritten custom.

Or somewhere in between.

The buffs, to-a-man, were driven to neurotic distraction by the mid-film munch of a Mars Bar or, worst of all, the maddening crinkle-crunch of a packet of crisps. After several foyer discussions about how best to react, a consensual decision was reached that a shake of the finger, heavy frown and silently mouthed 'Not allowed!' combined maximum effect with minimal disturbance of the screening. Which was fine until Brian's dodgy stomach began to gurgle, making more noise than the biscuit-nibbler he had admonished three seats away, sniggering now at her complainant's embarrassment. Anonymity remained an integral part of his pleasure in going to the cinema and drawing any kind of attention to himself was anathema. Fear for the echoing gurgle of his ill-behaved intestines made Brian anxious, which meant it was more likely to happen.

With the existence of the other buffs as moral support, pleased that no special involvement was expected either way, Brian dealt with these minor issues in life with a level of equanimity unknown to him before. He looked at film, wrote in his notebooks about what he had seen and thought, talked to the regulars, and worked quietly away at his rates desk during the day. As a BFI member Brian was entitled to advance booking on publication of each monthly schedule, normally six weeks ahead, and over an extra-long lunch at Lorenzo's on the same day the guide had arrived at home in the post, he made his decisions, telephoning them through from the office immediately that same afternoon. The sense of security experienced on noting the titles and times of a whole month's movie bookings in his diary was immeasurable. It had never occurred to Brian that he might one day feel such contentment.

As the years passed, he began to see films for the second time, revisiting favourite scenes, such as a particular shot in Hugh Hudson's *Chariots of Fire*, when the Harold Abrahams character was strolling lost in thought on his own along the towpath of the Cam, stopped and leaned his forehead against the fissured trunk of an oak, the similarly shaped profiles of human and tree facing each other, dual symbols of determination. Brian was pleased to be seeing the film again, re-screened by the BFI to register the sensational death of Dodi Fayed, the movie's executive producer. None of the buffs knew quite what to make of things, either of the national outpouring of grief for the loss of Princess Diana or about her luxury affair with Fayed and their high-speed accident in a Paris underpass.

Bahraini, wasn't he? someone asked.

Egyptian, another of the regulars corrected. Once married to an American actress, Suzanne Gregard. And divorced eight months later.

Mind you, I prefer *Breaking Glass*, which Fayed also produced, another buff commented.

In no time Brian had been ten years a buff, which he celebrated by catching an Ichikawa movie he had not had the chance to see before, *Tokyo Olympiad*, commissioned by the Organizing Committee of the 1964 Olympics, screened in a restored print to mark the current Winter Olympic Games held in Nagano. As Brian had hoped of Ichikawa, the film was as much about the fears and regrets as the triumphs, with the spectators and coaches and family friends given their human place alongside the competitors.

Film, not a sports report, he commented to fellow buffs after the screening.

Sportsmen the stars in Japan these days. Used to be the great directors, someone said. You know a Japanese athlete won gold in the ski jump last week?

Brian certainly did not know this, nor was he interested to hear. Ichikawa was hero enough for him.

He liked the sound of certain places as well as filmmakers. The other day he had booked in to see *Edge of Seventeen* simply because it was set in somewhere enticingly called Sandusky, Ohio, the name of the town the best thing about the new movie, it had turned out.

On his way one early evening from a cup of tea in the Royal Festival Hall café through to the BFI Brian noticed posters for an arts event to be held out on the riverfront:

FREE. Saturday 7th of August 1999 from 2.00pm to 9.00pm on the South Bank. THE ARTICULTURAL SHOW. Come to the open-air hybrid pop culture extravaganza. Sheep welcome.

Being on a weekend he decided to give it a try and on the designated afternoon came in early for his film.

The first stall Brian came upon was headlined *The Miracle of Holy Balls*, with a crucifix to which were attached by string a pair of realistically carved and painted wooden testicles, to be fondled on payment of a small fee in the fair's exclusive Sheep currency.

Brian resisted the temptation.

Next along was *The Rat Race*, in which five well-fed kittens displayed a sleepy reluctance to run down the walled lanes on a long tabletop, forcing the artist-stallholder to call off the race and return the punters' bets. And so the art-fun went on. Brian had never seen anything like it. Someone in a hairy gorilla suit pranced around the place daring passers-by to pin a beard onto his chin, the human creature's reaction unpredictable. There was a *Champagne and Sperm Bank*, its purpose and practice a mystery. Brian felt encouraged to stay longer at the show on finding that one of the artists was a superb puff pastry maker – he ordered two more of her pear and honey tartlets and a second mug of tea to savour at a sheltered table by the river. From this vantage point he observed in amusement the antics of *Jessica Voorsanger's Fanogram 2*, at which a mob of female art students rushed screaming over to some unsuspecting man and pleaded for his autograph, instructed to pretend he was a famous person, the name they shouted chosen and paid for and the victim selected by a bystander. During the time Brian was there he heard screams twice for 'Damien Hirst' and once each of 'Arsène Wenger', 'Sean Connery' and 'Fidel Castro'. He left for the BFI before the marshalling of audience participation in a staged performance of the Jonestown mass suicide, in which nine hundred cult followers had died drinking cyanide-spiked tea. Flyers distributed amongst the stalls assured the public that the event would be perfectly safe, more like a Sealed Knot re-enactment than horror movie. It was pointed out in the flyer that the correct name of this sorry site of deceit was The Peoples Temple Agricultural Project, shortened by the media to Jonestown after the instigator, Pentecostal preacher Jim Jones.

To Brian the most extraordinary occurrence during the first decade of his every-evening visits to the BFI was the incremental formation of what he had come to accept as friendship. It was not possible for him to be certain because in the self-inflicted solitude of his adult life he had never known anyone he could convincingly call a friend and therefore had nothing with which to compare this novel experience. There were one or two people whom he regularly saw, and was pleased so to do, such as Lorenzo at Il Castelletto, or Joe the barber, and, to a certain extent, Mr Wilson in the office, but these contacts were limited to single areas of his life, different from what he imagined real friendship might be. His potential friend, tall and angular, was the buffs' de facto leader, due to the longevity of his commitment to watching film – over twenty years an intermittent regular – and respected for the consequent depth of his knowledge as the group's authority on two subjects: the composers of movie scores and the history of early Indian cinema. The other buffs claimed expertise in a single topic at the most, Brian's reputation by then established for dependable information on classic Japanese film. His would-be friend was gentle, pale-faced, with untidy grey-brown hair falling in loose waves to his shoulders, and large spectacles resting on the bridge of a bony nose.

It transpired that outside the chosen anonymity of their group the man answered to a name: Jack.

Looking back Brian suspected that a distinct prospect of friendship had surfaced after he nominated the person he now knew as Jack, seconded with alacrity by several others, to co-curate a one-a-night slot for a month of Buffs' Choice, as the BFI programmers christened this special new series. The overwhelming majority of people invited to name a film, Brian had noticed in the brochure when printed, were professionals, festival organizers and critics and BFI employees, few authentic amateur buffs. He felt cheated, led down the garden path was the phrase echoing inside his head as he hurried to the South Bank on the first night of the new season – though he did feel it was good that the BFI had at least taken note of the regulars' vote for Jack and then selected one of his recommendations to open the season, *Shirley Valentine*, scripted by Willy Russell from his own play, a Lewis Gilbert movie admired at the time of release though not often seen in the ten years since. Reading Jack's programme notes, Brian recognized his fellow buff's approach to film, enjoyed his tenor and tone, warm and engaged, loving, even.

Jack had structured his printed comments around a quotation from a soliloquy in the film delivered by the main character, Shirley Valentine, a housewife in Wallasey at the mouth of the Mersey: 'I've led such a little life, and even that will be over very soon.'

Although Brian fancied he knew quite a bit about

Liverpool – on film, that is – it had not occurred to him that scouse humour possessed a twist of Jewish melancholy to it, as Jack had pointed out in the information sheet.

Russell, who was Liverpudlian himself, knew the right voice.

Was Tom Conti part-Greek?

He sounded to Brian exactly like he imagined a Mykonos taverna-owner would, the part he played in the movie. Not bad for a lad born and brought up in Paisley by a pair of Scottish hairdressers.

On further thought, Brian recalled other clever mimics on film. Look at Rampling, an Essex girl who spoke French like a native. Or ultra-English Jeremy Irons's clipped Danish lilt as the sinister Claus von Bulow.

Mind you, they are actors, Brian said afterwards in the foyer. It's their job.

One night on his way between cinema and tube, Brian became aware of a man's long strides drawing closer behind him and heard someone call his name. He turned around. It could only have been Jack. And there he was, in his grubby thigh-length windcheater, carrying the usual heavy duty Tesco shopping bag. Brian waited for him to catch up and they walked on together, enthusing about Alison Steadman, a key figure in the *Shirley Valentine* cast, whose acting both of them had also admired in *The Adventures of Baron Munchausen*, despite the film's panning by the critics.

Even better in *A Private Function*, Brian added.

Which looked as if it might have been made, but was not, by Mike Leigh, Steadman's husband, he was tempted to say but resisted overdoing things in the one-on-one presence of an authority of Jack's standing.

At the top of the steps to Waterloo Station Jack halted,

to ask Brian if he might agree to skip a night at the BFI the following Thursday to attend a concert with him next door at the Queen Elizabeth Hall, of contemporary film music, including two short pieces by Toru Takemitsu.

What an odd suggestion!

Tempting, though, as Takemitsu had composed the music, distinctive and original, for several of Brian's most prized Japanese movies – *Woman of the Dunes*, *Ran* and *Kwaidan,* for starters. His first thought was concern about the price of the ticket, unfamiliar with concert costs. On second thoughts, if Jack was able to afford it Brian was sure he could too.

He promised to think about it and to have decided by the time they met up the next night at the BFI. Brian declined, as he spoke, to look Jack in the eye, fearful in certain lights of seeing his own face reflected on the curved surface of another's cornea and finding himself unable to resist the magnetic power of alien control. Wary in general of eyes, he was caught up for a random moment in a zombie story and forgot it was Jack's kind gaze he was facing.

The two went off on their separate ways home, Jack to Tooting and Brian to Kentish Town. By the time the tube train had passed a couple of stations Brian had silenced his horror fantasies and decided to say yes.

Over coffee in the curved vestibule of the Queen Elizabeth Hall before the concert Brian learnt that Jack quite often attended performances of film-related music, particularly on visits to London by renowned Indian musicians. Transported from the set habits of their cinema-going, the conversation flew disturbingly free, Brian discovering that Jack worked for an Iranian travel agent in Streatham, in the backroom, forbidden from handling customers direct, and that he was the father of a daughter whom he had not seen or heard of since her tenth birthday, twenty-six years ago. The mother, his then wife, was a teacher and Jack was surprised, he said, that she had put up with him for as long as she did.

There were no reciprocal revelations from Brian.

As the concert hall was only half full, shortly before the start they moved down from their cheaper seats near the back to a partly vacant row in the rear stalls while the musicians of the London Sinfonietta tuned their instruments, first woodwind then the strings, in front of an impressive array of percussion and two synthesizers, the latter players absent for the first piece. Tuning complete, the hall fell silent, awaiting the arrival of the conductor.

Waiting rather a long time, Brian felt, and looked anxiously at Jack to check if something had gone wrong.

Jack smiled and mouthed, here he is.

Moving slowly from backstage left came a tall man all in black, overweight, with full beard. On reaching the rostrum he gave the briefest bow to the audience, turned towards the orchestra, raised his white baton and set the music in instant motion. The delicacy of sound drawn from his musicians by this huge amorphous figure jolted Brian into unanticipated respect and he let out an involuntary sigh. At which Jack handed him an open programme, pointing with his dirty fingernail to the composer's name and the title of the piece being performed, *Atmosphères - 2001: A Space Odyssey* by György Ligeti.

Not quite the same as the film score, was it? Brian commented in the interval. Great, though. Could almost see the sun rise in outer space!

So measured, Jack said. Even better with a full-size symphony orchestra.

It was altogether a terrific concert, they both agreed. Brian found stimulating the opportunity, courtesy of

Jack, to hear music for film outside the cinema and intended to listen more attentively in future to the scores of movies at the BFI.

He did not have long to wait, grateful for the chance a few days later to see Oshima's *The Ceremony*, with a score by Takemitsu, the movie turning out to be an arcane succession of rites of family celebration and sorrow. Oshima was said to believe that the true spirit of Japan revealed itself in traditional ceremonies, a remark that Brian tried – with little success – to convince his sceptical fellow buffs was the point of the film. Near the end a character named Terumichi committed hara-kiri in a bare stone-walled hut on a distant island, where his betrothed eventually found his body stretched out face down at the foot of a wooden pole, naked, spattered in blood. She drew a slender knife from beneath her kimono and plunged it into her stomach, expiring at her lover's side. All of this to Takemitsu's refined modernist music.

Very Japanese, someone said, and everybody laughed, even Brian.

The previous evening the gathered buffs had laughed so loudly and for so long after seeing Corman's *The Trip*, almost controlling themselves and then collapsing again in hysterics, that the house manager had asked them to move outside to the riverfront. When he had calmed down sufficiently to complete a sentence, Brian had managed to say that the thing which he found irresistibly funny was the way the cast played themselves as if acting – Dennis Hopper, Peter Fonda, and Bruce Dern as the spoilt drugged-up hippies they were in real life, to a script by 'bad boy' Jack Nicholson and musical score by the soul rock band Electric Flag.

No wonder it made a fortune in the 1960s! Terrible film!

They had laughed some more and wandered off to catch bus, tube and train to their respective homes.

On a Saturday morning two weeks later, buoyed by the mutual pleasure of their evening at the concert, Brian found himself taking the underground south to Tooting Broadway to visit Jack, the declared purpose to look at his collection of film books. Despite diligently taking down the directions in his notebook, at the station Brian took the right bus in the wrong direction and had to get off, cross the road and wait for one going west towards Summerstown, ring the bell for the stop by the cemetery and walk down a meandering street towards Jack's place. Confused by the numbering of the half-doors in the shared porches of a terrace of diminutive houses, Brian was relieved when the bell he pressed proved correct. He beamed at Jack with greater warmth than intended, narrowly evading a hug.

Feeling uneasy, seated with a mug of coffee in Jack's tiny overheated front room, fitted bookshelves floor to ceiling on three walls, Brian wrestled to recover his sense of self-control. He grimaced, closed his eyes and told himself to behave, that he was visiting his first real friend and needed to calm down. Brian opened his eyes, glanced at the nearest shelf, pulled out a book at random and began, with genuine interest, to thumb the pages. The shadow of awkwardness between them lifted.

In the confined book-lined room they sat opposite each other in front of a fizzing gas fire, Jack's sallow face bathed in sunlight from the window, their feet almost touching. Brian noticed Jack frowning down at his shoes and followed his gaze to be made aware of the contrast between his friend's disintegrating camouflage trainers and his own black leather oxfords. It was sensible, Brian defensively told himself, to take care of shoes. His were nothing special, mid-range Freeman Hardy Willis the most he could afford at the time, three identical pairs in five-eye lace-up worn in sequence each for a single day to delay deterioration and moderate the smell from his inappropriately named athlete's foot. Brushed and polished, the two resting pairs stood in their plastic shoe trees beneath his bedroom chair. For wet winter weekends, when out and about on domestic errands and bookshop recces, Brian kept in lieu a pair of brown chukka boots, warm and dry. On cold Sunday mornings he wore a navy-blue mackintosh and under his jacket a V-neck sweater, plain blue. Brian's hard-working jackets quickly looked the worse for wear, crumpled out of shape by his fleshless bottom from the hours seated day and night in office and cinema. By contrast, beneath his solitary windcheater Jack only ever wore woollen pullovers, loose and long, two of them hand-knitted.

By whom?

His ex-wife? What was her name, Brian wondered.

He extracted himself from these silent thoughts about clothes and wives and asked Jack how far it was from Tooting to Streatham and his job at the travel agents.

Brian enjoyed their talk, Jack rising from his chair several times to extract from the shelves a movie book to illustrate a point. They mourned the imminent closure of the Museum of the Moving Image, barely eleven years after its opening was heralded with national coverage of the BFI's purchase at auction for £19,800 of Marilyn Monroe's lacy black dress from *Some Like it Hot*. Jack liked best at MOMI, he declared, the display of early optical devices, content to sit for ages turning the drum of the reproduction zoetrope to watch jugglers throw and catch coloured balls and runners passing the baton in a relay race. Brian admitted that, when no-one was looking, he slipped into the self-film booth to be recorded reading the *News at Ten*, then to watch himself split-screen interviewed by the film critic Barry Norman. It was fun, they agreed, hoping the money would somehow be found to reopen the museum.

For no particular reason, in an attempt at ordinary conversation, Brian asked Jack how he planned to mark the passing of the millennium, which had crept up along with the approaching end of the year

In Madagascar, to photograph the green sunset, came the unexpected reply.

A joke of some kind, Brian presumed.

On pursuing his friend into the kitchen – with a table, four wooden chairs and a frosted glass door leading to the tiny back yard – Brian was gratified to note that Jack's meticulous domestic arrangements contradicted the disorder of his personal dress and general demeanour. It transpired that both of them knew within a few drops the amount of water to boil economically in the kettle for a decent pot of tea, Kenyan loose leaf, Brian's from Sainsbury's, Jack's from Tesco. Brian noticed that Jack was a cold press juicer, with three glass bowls of different fruit lined up on the sideboard beside his Magimix Deluxe. As expected, no call for an ironing board, whereas Brian left his permanently unfolded at the far side of his bed, making the same number and direction of sweeps of his steam iron on the front and collar of each shirt, not bothering with the backs. Jack was devoted to his microwave, he said, best invention since the moving image.

There was no need at the end of the visit to make arrangements to meet up again, as they would do so anyway at the BFI.

Estranged for decades from his family, Brian had transferred his emotional loyalties to individual directors of film, their deaths mourned, bringing the ghost of a tear to his eye for several months afterwards as the credits rolled on work by a favourite deceased moviemaker. He found it tough to carry the sadness and loss, to accept that he would never again feel the excitement of waiting outside NFT 1 for a new film by the particular him or her. Brian was indifferent to gender and although there were fewer women directors in the movie business, he liked several and did not want any of them to die: Campion, of course; Bigelow was good too most of the time; Margarethe von Trotta's feminist explosions; and, above others, the gnomic fun of red-mop Varda, whom Brian willed to live forever.

There were one or two directors whose work Brian admired but found uncomfortable, intrinsically disturbing. Of these Federico Fellini was the most problematic. Brian sat at home with his mug of tea many-a-night after a Fellini movie at the BFI, trying to work out why he felt unspecified unease, usually deciding it was something about the wilful glee with which the director liked to upset assumptions. Nothing was safe from his raucous ridicule. Brian felt knocked off balance by Fellini, the familiar signposts of his life no longer legible, everything unstable.

There were no rational grounds for Brian to be troubled, as the subjects of Fellini's films were seldom of relevance to him personally.

What did he know or care about Rome, Brian asked himself.

Nothing.

He had never been, never dreamed of going, and yet *Roma*, a wild semi-documentary, had really disturbed him.

Gore Vidal hit the nail on the head when he said in the movie itself of the Eternal City: 'What better place is

50

there from which to watch the death of civilization?'

At home Brian felt vindicated in his views on reading in the programme notes a comment by the director himself: 'Vulgarity is part of the character of Rome, a kind of liberation, a victory over fear of bad taste, over propriety.'

And he chuckled on remembering what Jack had said some time ago about *Orchestra Rehearsal*, Fellini's deceptively light-hearted seventy-minute movie of the 1970s: 'As compact as a hand-grenade!'

One night recently he had not expected to be moved by Fellini's film about the fictional return to TV of a long-retired tap dancing couple and was caught by surprise with *Ginger and Fred*, wonderfully played by the director's wife Giulietta Masina and the star of many of his previous films, Marcello Mastroianni. In this case Brian was aware of the cause of his distress: chaotic disintegration in the ageing life of Mastroianni's character Fred, temporarily released from confinement in an asylum to take part in the television show, in which he danced with brave incompetence. Brian hated seeing Fred make a public fool of himself.

Jack had again made a pertinent comment at the buffs' gathering in the BFI foyer, that Mastroianni's white thinning hair and his wearing of Fellini's own topcoat, hat and scarf made deliberate reference to the director's own ageing, sixty-six at the time *Ginger and Fred* was made, seven years before his death from a heart attack.

On seeing some fifteen years after its release Yilmaz Güney's *The Wall*, Brian was shocked on the tube train home to read in the programme notes that the director was dead, struck down by gastric cancer in 1984, a year after completing *Duvar* – the crisper Turkish title, preferred by Brian. Delayed knowledge of Güney's death propelled Brian into awareness of the director's real-life

circumstances, instead of concentrating as he generally did on the filmed reality. Set in a child's prison near
Ankara with an all-Turkish cast, *Duvar* was in fact shot in
Germany, with non-actor children from refugee families
housed in West Berlin, opponents of the military. Güney
himself had found brief protection in Germany after
lengthy periods of imprisonment in Istanbul, condemned
for the political essence of the films he had insisted on
continuing to make. Brian took note in his book from an
interview with the director quoted by the BFI, Güney's
sentimental words lent a certain weight by the humanity
of his visual images:

> Since I left Turkey, all my books, all my films have been
> banned. It couldn't be otherwise. Because in this pitiless
> war, each one fights with his own arms. It is up to us to
> depict the realities of Turkey, so that they may finally
> change... Since I have openly expressed my opinions, I
> have not ceased to be hunted down. Living abroad today
> there is no change in my life, that is to say, I am still vigilant,
> but I'm not afraid. So long as I have the strength to de-
> nounce and fight fascism I will do so.

Whenever – quite often, usually on weekend mornings
– Brian began to feel self-conscious about the limited life
he led, berating himself for lacking political, religious or
any other firm belief, and finding unforgiveable his lack
of social responsibility for anybody else, all he could
think of doing was to close the doors of his mind yet tight-
er against everything other than film. There was no point
in questioning his choices now.

It was too late for doubt, much too late.

Before despair could take hold, Brian had been able,
to date, to remind himself that the reason why he was a

regular at the BFI was because it made him feel part of something outside, a player in a very small way on the world stage of cinema. Reading that Güney said it was 'up to us', Brian's blood tingled with conviction, in the sense that he felt peripherally one of 'us', a singular essential element, the committed viewer of film, a member of the audience. Without people like him to watch it, film did not exist and the brave work of directors like Güney, Loach, Kiarostami, and other politically motivated artists would be meaningless.

Brian felt comforted by the memory of a private conversation with Jack, during which he had refused point blank to answer a personal question about Ireland, prompting Jack to say something wise and kind: that there were certain things which everyone had best keep to themselves, unspoken. Even filmmakers have secrets, Jack had said, personal experiences never to be told.

While it felt good to have spent time with Jack outside the cinema, Brian remained vulnerable to disproportionate distress at alteration to his routine, as happened not long after his Saturday trip to Tooting. With no room for a washing machine in his kitchenette, once a fortnight on a Sunday morning Brian took his pillowcase of dirty clothes and bed linen to the launderette a couple of blocks down Kentish Town Road. He liked going, enjoyed his regular chat with the woman who looked after the place, on a recent visit commiserating with her over an accident with self-tanning ointment, blotching her legs below the knee. She insisted he look and, it being her, he had, reluctantly.

He liked the warm heavy air of the launderette and its enveloping mechanical sounds, and strolled over from his flat with anticipated pleasure.

'CLOSED FOR THE DAY. SORRY' it said on a magic-marker notice stickered to the inside of the window. After standing there for several minutes in disarray, shifting from foot to foot, Brian trudged back home to hand-wash necessities in the bath. Upset by the disruption to his routine, Brian needed reassurance that things remained in order in the flat, and stood in front of his kitchen cupboards, closed his eyes and opened a door, reaching sightless towards the spot where the sugar bowl was meant to be.

And there it was!

While rinsing his underclothes and laying them out to dry on the padded coat of the hot water tank, Brian resurrected the comfort-memory of two films about launderettes.

The first was an art video he had seen at the BFI some weeks ago in the London Film Festival's night of shorts, *Laundromat-Locomotion* by the inventive Steven Pippin. Brian remembered watching with open-mouthed disbelief Pippin's muted colour footage of a red-coated huntsman on horseback cantering through the double doors from the street and past a row of twelve washing machines that the artist had earlier in the film been shown converting to the unlikely task of taking and developing photographs. Towards the end of the video these black and white images were shown close-up, the rider and horse distorted through the machines' round windows with scuffs of use and spots of debris. Brian had chased up in the BFI archives an earlier Pippin video, *The Continued Saga of an Amateur Photographer*, of the artist locked in the loo of a train travelling from London to Brighton, filmed in the process of converting the lavatory to take and develop photographs. He took off his suit trousers to black-out the toilet bowl to develop the film. Brian appreciated Pippin's deadpan supply of the technical information in the twenty-minute video, edited from the continuous 16mm film shot from a mini-camera taped to the ceiling of the toilet of British Rail Carriage No.7680, the sixth photographic toilet-exposure taking place at 12.32 p.m., shortly before arrival in Brighton. Pippin quickly packed away his equipment in a briefcase, adjusted his tie and joined the platform crowd like an innocent commuter.

Brian's feature movie memory of washing machines was of Daniel Day-Lewis in his break-through role of Johnny Burfoot in *My Beautiful Laundrette*, with rocker-blond streaks in his hair and expressive tongue.

Thinking about the central relationship in *My Beautiful Laundrette*, Brian found himself reaffirming in his head dislike of the term bisexual, or indeed asexual. It was the sound and look of the words he objected to, and the veiled disapproval, rather than the meanings. His own sexuality was a matter of unconcern to Brian – bi or nei, he used to say to himself, nei being his abbreviated term for neither. Providing they left him alone, he was indifferent as to how people ascribed his sexual leanings. Made aware from over-excited Christmas parties in the office that he was seen as a closet homosexual, he did not mind at all, providing nobody called him gay. Certainly not to his face and preferably not amongst themselves. He hated labels.

If pushed, Brian thought of himself as sexually suppressed in matters of action while opinionated and observant when it came to sex on film, not in the sense of physical stimulus, unconcerned with turn-on or sexiness in general, fascinated instead by the narrative techniques of screen sex. In his study of the topic Brian had developed a system for categorizing the different types of cinematic failure to portray convincingly the act and emotions of intimacy. In life's interactions with fellow buffs or at work and in chance encounters in street or café, he stifled feelings of sexual interest before they might emerge, self-withdrawn from the prospect of closeness. The pleasure he had felt on his distant decision to remain chaste and live alone had been so immediate that he had since forgotten what physical arousal felt like, liberated to a cool-eyed critique of sexuality on film, delighted to be free from the threat of personal complications in connection to fellow buffs. Though Brian cared what his friends at the BFI thought of him as a human-being and also, of course, of his judgement of film, he gave no thought as to how they might or might not assess him sexually. He was uninterested, unavailable, and that was it.

For the time being, certainly.

Even more so at work, his personal interest in colleagues negative, less than nil.

The single communal work event which Brian enjoyed, the Camden Housing Office summer outing to Chessington World of Adventures, came round again. In the past they used to take a riverboat down the Thames for the half-day, a horror trip for Brian, trapped for hours with a load of heedless drinkers. On one outing the karaoke in the saloon was so loud and relentless he would have jumped overboard, if only he could swim. He had mostly managed to invent excuses not to go. Though Mr Wilson had once caught him out, more amused than angry when he had claimed – evidently for the second time – attendance at his non-existent godfather's funeral. After the zoo at Chessington expanded in the late 1980s into a theme park, the office had switched venues for its day out. It was the kind of place with many activities in which Brian felt free to participate or not, dependent on how the others were behaving, usually joining the gang on the rollercoaster water chute, where he and they opened their mouths wide and screamed, like ponderous children. Over a number of annual visits Brian had grown attached to a larger-than-life mural on the boundary wall, of a lush blonde, eyes closed as she kissed a tiger on its black nose.

Brian used to stand transfixed in front of the colourfully painted mural, picturing himself kissing the girl, a rare instance of his sexual fantasizing.

The other star attraction for Brian was the Wall of Death, a wide wooden drum down into which the audience gazed from circular rows of raked benches above, at motorcyclists riding faster and faster until parallel to the ground. One rider in a cowboy hat somehow stood horizontal on the machine's saddle and held his arms above his head.

There was a café at Chessington which Brian liked, where he made sure to leave plenty of time for tea before the Council's coach departed on return to Central London. Sitting in the sun with a daring iced coffee and slice of cheesecake, he felt peaceful enough to remember his mother and their summer daytrips on the train to Margate, with its smaller fairground and broad curved beach. The only thing missing at the World of Adventures was candyfloss, which he used to beg his mother to buy for him even though he never really enjoyed the sticky pink mess.

Mr Wilson had developed the habit of meeting up with Brian at the café for a concluding cup of tea.

Nothing to beat the Ghost Train, Wilson said.

It's the Wall of Death for me, Brian responded, aware that this was what they both almost always said to each other towards the end of their annual day at Chessington. He liked the repeating pattern and had grown to feel relatively relaxed with his tubby bald boss, who customarily ordered a towering ice cream sundae topped with syrup and maraschino cherries.

In an expansive mood, feeling good about himself, Brian decided to return to the West Ham stadium for the first time since his aborted attempt to become a football supporter, this time on Bloomsday, for a gala performance of Riverdance and curated feast of Joycean memorabilia. Brian had not actually read any of James Joyce's books, attendance at the Bloomsday event a peripheral form of acknowledging his Irish heritage for once. Lord-of-the-dance Flatley and his troupe of black-stockinged girls were an irrelevance, as far as Brian was concerned.

The quote from *Finnegan's Wake* which Brian often repeated to himself, 'roll away the reel world', he had taken down from a BFI programme note.

He read somewhere that Eisenstein had discussed with Joyce the possibility of their making a film together!

Of the several inevitably flawed films related to *Ulysses*, the only attempts which Brian liked were Rossellini's *Voyage to Italy* of 1954 and Huston's intimate *The Dead*, taken from a short story and released in 1987, four months after the director's death.

Jack, who had read a fair amount of the fiction, shared Brian's view of Joyce in the cinema, whilst also retaining a soft spot for John Gielgud as The Preacher in Strick's *A Portrait of the Artist as a Young Man*.

Better informed about early picture houses than literature, Brian was aware that in 1909 Joyce had formally opened the first public movie house in Dublin, the Volta Electric. Not long ago the altered theatre had been demolished, replaced by a Primark shopping complex, making extra-special to Brian his postcards of the original Volta, with an elaborate street frieze financed by Italian friends of the writer.

Irritated by the recorded cod-Irish music to which

Riverdance performed on their spectacularly lit temporary stage at the North Bank of the West Ham ground, Brian made his way back through the cheering crowd on the pitch to the far end, past a clutch of stalls, one selling black eye patches printed with a circular spectacle lens and another flogging Leopold and Molly Bloom dolls in compromising poses. For a mad moment Brian thought of buying a black bowler hat, before sensibly deciding against the idea. Near the end of the ground the banner 'Learn To Line Dance' was slung across the entrance to a large marquee. He went inside to see what was happening, and a curly-haired Irish girl took him immediately by the arm, ushering him towards the registration table. Brian managed to make her stop and listen while he explained that he had never, even as a boy in Belfast, been able to keep step with the marching bands, his legs deaf to rhythm. Halted in her market stride, the girl for the first time properly attended to the mild middle-aged man she had hijacked. She smiled amiably, and patted him on the bum, as if still a boy in the band.

Take care, she said, before moving off in search of less inhibited customers.

For no obvious reason, Brian was reminded of Jack speaking the other day about the evening he had spent in The Eagle pub in Farringdon at a concrete poetry and sound performance by Birdyak, with a tenor saxophonist and two voice-benders.

A right hoot, Jack had said. They did a shout duet of Bush and that young Putin putting signatures to their Strategic Offensive Reductions treaty!

Brian chuckled at the memory of Jack's description, recalling also the film he had seen the week before, adapted from the earlier B.S. Johnson novel *Christie Malry's Own Double-Entry*, about the extraction of self-assessed recompense from the State for the miseries of ordinary life. Christie, a clerk in West London, first built a toy train with which to deliver a bomb to raze the local tax offices to the ground and then poisoned a nearby reservoir, killing off 200,000 more-or-less innocent citizens.

Somewhat excessive, Brian said to himself, with a shrug.

The controlled parameters of Brian's life left little room for wider world events to impinge. The atrocities and rebellions and things which he read about in the newspaper occurred at a distance, in his perception, and tended to affect him directly only when channelled through film. This happened on seeing a new Vietnam War movie, *We Were Soldiers* directed by Randall Wallace and starring Mel Gibson, situated near the beginning of armed American involvement in the conflict between North and South Vietnam, leading up to the bloody Battle of Ia Drang Valley and the death of over half the US troops on the ground at the time.

Standard for the genre, nothing special in Brian's judgement, the usual graphic close-ups of bayonets and bullets piercing flesh, phosphorous grenades exploding in faces and napalm removing layers of skin.

On his way home on the tube, he found himself growing steadily angrier at the film's pretensions, the lavish re-creation – for entertainment – of war's vile reality. The more authentic a film attempted to be the more false in effect it was. The enactment of actuality was by definition a deceit, Brian felt, deliberate and damaging. Especially when live-war was being waged at that very moment with American and British troops right then rampaging through Iraq, blowing up schools and hospitals, bombing power stations, devastating an Arab country twice the size of Great Britain.

60

Brian's normal routine on reaching home at night was to make a pot of tea, briefly read a film magazine, take a long hot bath and go to bed. Instead he switched on the television to watch the news, and caught the Prime Minister rabbiting on about the allies' urgent search for Saddam's weapons of mass destruction. And for Saddam Hussein himself, who had somehow slipped free of the encircling net.

There goes Intelligence!

The only WMD which existed, Jack had said, was Bush and Blair's Willingness to Murder the Defenceless.

Brian scratched his nose.

Worse than *We Were Soldiers*.

Sitting thoughtfully at his desk, Brian lifted out his current notebook from his soft leather bag. At least half the notes he took down were on Japanese films, the description of minor happenings on screen that he might otherwise forget. Unusually for Brian, incensed by Gibson's melodramatic acting followed now by Blair's blind self-assurance, he wrote slowly to himself, crossing out words and replacing them until content with the sentences' sense:

> Seduced by the sound of their own voices, politicians
> choose not to care that their utterances cause actual death
> around the world. Of hundreds of thousands of people
> most years, one way and another.

On writing this down and closing the notebook, Brian felt his anger soften, both about the film and the Prime Minister, and he ran himself a hot bath.

Given the craven state of international public affairs, Brian felt warmed inside at having found a place for himself close to the centre of the BFI band of cinema devotees, and this despite his aversion to certain of their habits – such as carrying around battered plastic shopping bags, handles twisted and stretched, logos sagging. Brian found himself in his darker moods doubting the visual taste of anybody tolerating the perpetual company of the blue, red and white insignia of a Tesco's grocery bag.

What weight could he honestly attach to such a man's discernment?

It distressed Brian to think like this. He felt guilty registering an aesthetic shudder at the sight of the dandruff and strands of straggly mouse-grey hair on the shoulders of Jack's windcheater, eyes magnified behind his outsized spectacles.

As soon as such thoughts arose, Brian regretted giving space to things he could do nothing about, indeed about which nothing needed doing. He was being unfair and petty. The buffs centred their attention on how films looked not on how they did themselves, over-used carrier bags a price worth paying for Jack's amiable companionship.

In a tangential form of apology for his ungenerous reflections, Brian followed Jack's advice to see *Piravi*, praised by him for its lush green portrayal of the southern Indian state of Kerala, with a wonderful score based on traditional music of the countryside. An old man waited at the village bus stop day after day for the promised return of his student son from college in Trivandrum, the state capital. Brian breathed deep with pleasure at the slow rural pace of the film, noting afterwards from the BFI programme that the composer, Govindan Aravindan, was also from Trivandrum, which helped explain the intimate bond between sound and image. The son never arrived and his sister agreed on behalf of their father to take the bus into the city to find out what had happened, discovering that he had been implicated in student protests and had died by accident in a police cell.

Jack had gone to a different film, which had ended earlier, and Brian was prevented from immediately thanking him for the recommendation. It was a lovely film, and moving, to Brian, who felt for the rural family's loss of their clever son, caught up in the violence of national politics, thus drawing down the wrath of authority.

Both Jack and Brian were amongst the band of buffs who turned up at the weekend for unveiling to the public of NFT 3, in what used to be the Museum of the Moving Image's theatre for the projection of historic movies, the entire MOMI enterprise now permanently abandoned. The building was still in transition, and they trekked along makeshift passages and up half cut-off flights of stairs to the wide luxury seats and technical excellence of the auditorium, most of the buffs applauding the BFI's choice of *Bicycle Thieves* to open the programme.

At their huddle afterwards in the entrance foyer, the buffs' Italian specialist was attended to with interest as he described in detail the process by which Vittorio De Sica had elicited, so soon after the end of the war, such amazing performances from his non-professional cast. It was only the second time Brian had seen this classic film, put off at his first viewing ten years earlier by what he had then perceived to be its sentimentality. This time round he had taken to it differently, struck near the beginning by the symbolic repression in the concrete brutalism of the apartment block where the boy and his parents lived, chill and bare, like dwelling on the moon. Later in the film he had felt viscerally the physical danger of threatening crowds, initially to the father and then also to the young son.

Bicycle Thieves, he decided, deserved its place in the canon.

All his life, everywhere he went, Brian had shunned attention, the scars unhealed from being singled out at school in Kent as different and blamed for being so, by teachers, by other boys and by his mother. To ease this hurt he had made himself an expert at forgetting, a skill by now matured, able most of the time to erase unwelcome thoughts and happenings. It did mean that he needed to hold himself on constant alert, ready to combat the threat of being taken by surprise, a state-of-being he had managed to achieve without the tension driving him crazy. There had been costs, by now discounted and removed from memory. The increasing curvature of his spine was one, outbreaks of eczema another. Accompanying the physical reactions to Brian's taut self-discipline, the mental and emotional strains were easier, he found, to suppress, to pretend did not exist. All of which helped explain why Brian had adapted unquestioningly to nightly visits to the BFI, by which he was enabled, he felt, to escape his destiny of defeat.

A gala revival screening of *Dakota Road* concisely illustrated why Brian was so pleased to be a film buff.

Early into one of his favourite seats, on the aisle towards the back of the left-hand block in NFT 1, Brian felt a glow of well-being and, contrary to his normal practice of passive compliance, sought to work out the reason why. Which was obvious, once he dared to look. Because, as he had told himself before but repeatedly needed reminding, in the cinema he disappeared as a person and was accepted as a member of the crowd, an indistinguishable presence at an event of public significance, in this case the retrospective celebration of a promising director's first film.

Put differently, Brian felt almost as if he was being welcomed home.

As the theatre began to fill Brian listened to the chatter of the crowd calling and waving to each other across the rows, indicating that many had been involved in production of the film, reunited for this special performance. A BFI programmer whose name Brian did not quite catch, a joyous woman in colourful striped tights, introduced the director-writer Nick Ward and he in his turn introduced the film, straightway explaining that Dakota referred not to the Midwest of America but to a US airbase in an isolated spot in the Norfolk Fens, where the film was set. Brian was grateful to a member of the audience calling out to say she could not hear properly, as neither could he, and the curator and director swopped microphones. Which was good, as Ward had interesting things to say, suggesting that his film was in essence about networks of hidden desire and the damage these cause to both victim and perpetrator. Brian was taken aback by the emotional turn of the director's concluding remarks, stating that he had made *Dakota Road* for people like himself: 'Coping with the general business of living, and feeling that so many others find life easy, or at least give the impression of doing so.'

On viewing the film and admiring the affectionate portrait of the countryside, Brian assumed the director must have grown up in the flatlands of East Anglia, and was surprised to learn he was born on Corio Bay in the hinterland of Geelong, in South Australia.

Brian was often wrong-footed by films set in the British landscape, where he took recognition for granted, illogically, as he had seen in actuality very little of it. In a programme of eight avant garde classics, he had once seen a short film made in 1975 by a young graduate from the Slade School of Art, shot on the northern slopes of Mount Carningly in Wales, at one frame every twenty seconds from sunrise to sunset over seven consecutive days. None of the other buffs were in the Studio that night, having chosen other movies to watch, and Brian had no-one to talk to, to decode together the mechanical camera mounting required to achieve such other-worldly effects. He was mystified, and impressed.

His deliberate separation of cinema from life outside meant that however moved or frightened Brian was by a movie, his own uneventful existence was seldom affected. On watching *Testament*, for example, Lynne Littman's film on nuclear disaster, Brian had been horrified by its emotional conviction and by the tense portrayal of human suffering. In the years since he had quite often thought of it as a film, in admiration, without, however, transferring the narrative fearfulness into his external day. When Littman's short documentary *Testament at 20* was screened the week before *Dakota Road*, Brian had gone to see it eagerly and was pleased to hear from the actors interviewed on camera, as well as from the director, how powerfully the film had been received at the original screening twenty years earlier, the first feature on nuclear threat to be made by a woman director. What distressed Brian was not nuclear horror but the fact that this documentary was the last film Littman would ever make, due to the deterioration of her sight through near blindness in her hooded left eye.

She was sixty-two, only seven years older than him.

How could she contemplate life without making films?

Impossible.

He would fall down dead, he knew he would, if unable

to see cinema.

Brian constantly came across on film world-things of which he was debilitatingly ignorant. One of the advantages of mostly watching older movies was to catch up on information missing from his blinkered existence. Towering above its rivals in this respect was *Shoah*, which had altered Brian's understanding of the holocaust, a film nine hours long and eleven years in the making. He had winced at the director Claude Lanzmann's relentless questioning on film of ageing Polish witnesses of the capture and extermination of Jews in the 1940s and felt sorry for these low-paid farmers and factory workers trapped in inarticulate habits of denial. Lanzmann pressed on and on, angrier and more self-righteous by the hour, unable most of the time to secure admission of guilt. It was irrational to pity these tacit collaborators in such dreadful acts, but Brian could not help himself, touched by the hurt in their stubborn faces.

A hand-held camera walked the cinema audience through fertile green pastures, guided to what a now-old Jewish survivor believed to be the site, as accurately as he could remember the revulsion of that time, where he had been forced to pile into a pit hundreds of the rotting corpses of his fellow inmates from the concentration camp.

Ghettos and cattle trucks Brian had known about. What he had never seen before were the Polish villages in the countryside around Auschwitz, the lanes and gardens, even some of the houses themselves little changed from the days when smoke wafted down from the crematoria chimneys, smelling like glue.

Midnight Cowboy was another revelation, in a different way, an emotive two-step around vagrant life in New York.

Brian liked these contrasts from night to night at the

BFI. It kept him on his toes, he maintained.

Not only the subject of *Midnight Cowboy* surprised him, the vocabulary too.

Ratso and the hustler. Terrific!

It had not previously occurred to Brian that there was a living to be earned serving rich needy women of a certain age.

Not by him, of course.

Nor by the Voigt character either, the movie revealed.

His ridiculous hat and perpetual open-mouthed buck-teeth chewing of gum. No wonder he failed.

In successive brief fantasies, after seeing *Midnight Cowboy* Brian became a shoeshiner, after *Babette's Feast* a cook, after *One Flew Over the Cuckoo's Nest* a strong silent Cherokee, after *Three Colours Blue* Juliette Binoche's aunt, after *Mean Streets* a New York gangster, after *Daddy Nostalgie* a dying invalid, after *The Herd* a shepherd, after *Mephisto* an actor, and after *Mirror* a paternal poet. Endless substitutions for an inadequate self.

In a back issue of *Sight & Sound,* Brian was irritated to read a description of *Mean Streets* as 'remarkable for its moral realism – realism without cynicism'.

Really!

Why not say that Scorsese's characters felt like actual people, from any era, flawed and vulnerable?

On his next free Saturday morning Brian visited the cinema bookshop off Ladbroke Grove, with its solid stock of new as well as second-hand books on film, pleased to purchase a copy of Faber & Faber's screenplay of *Dakota Road*, as mentioned by the BFI lady. He liked the cover, in line with other paperbacks in the series, designed with a stylized clapperboard above the black-and-white title box. Admiration of this graphic detail had enticed Brian to purchase in the past more Faber film books than he could properly afford. Including the weighty volume of Truffaut's letters which he had read from cover to cover, all 580 pages. It was comforting, he found, to learn of the French director's contrariness, unequivocal in the claim that his refusal to learn was as powerful as his wish to know. There was so much of interest to Brian in this series of books. In her preface to Satyajit Ray's *My Years with Apu*, the director's widow wrote of her sorrow at the theft from the nursing home during her husband's dying days of the altered and expanded version of this posthumously published draft, his annotated text never recovered.

Done with browsing, Brian hurried around the corner to the Turkish café he always visited on West London book-outings and as soon as he sat down began to thumb Ward's script.

He stopped suddenly and looked up. Not at anything in the café, at something which had appeared in his head, the realization that Truffaut's remembered remark applied to him too, that his contradictory purpose in watching film was to escape from the world and at the same time learn about it.

On finishing his second cup of tea and a slice of walnut baklava, Brian checked his watch and realized there was time to take a detour from his customary route and pass by the Electric Cinema on Portobello Road, which had recently closed down, bankrupt again, for the umpteenth time. His collection of postcards of early cinemas included three of the Electric, hand-coloured in the lithographic plate: of the street perspective, the box office foyer, and the auditorium. As he had never before been to see the building itself, Brian stood in concentration on the opposite side of the road gazing above the fruit and vegetable stalls at the asymmetric arch, lead-lined dome and gratuitous relief swags. He reckoned, from memory of his shoebox of postcards at home in the flat, that relatively little had changed since publication of the original postcards soon after the Electric Cinema Theatre's first public screening in 1911. Such a determined survivor, he hoped it would reopen again soon.

Brian treasured the banner names of early cinemas: the Pyramid in Sale, the People's Electric in West Drayton, Clements Pictures in Skegness, Gale's Bioscope Show in Stratford, the Clapton Cinematograph in Hackney, the Angel Picture Theatre in Islington, Pringle's Picture Palace in Edinburgh, original postcards of all of which he owned.

Names made all the difference.

What possible chance did he, a Brian, have of public acclaim?

How could Arnold Schwarzenegger fail with a name, body and ambition like his, however limited in talent?

Brian had his doubts about Marlon Brando as an ace name, whilst convinced all the same by the quality of the man as an actor.

Last Tango in Paris, now there was a tip-top performance, which had propelled Brian to the edge of his seat for the entire film.

At least the name of Brando's birthplace had a ring to it: Omaha, Nebraska.

In an utterly unpredictable intervention three days later Brian found himself slowly, hazily struggling for consciousness in a crowded hospital ward. There was something wrong with his head. He released an arm from the tightly folded bedclothes and reached up to touch what felt like a turban, covering his ears and also restricting his sight. The muffling of sound in the busy

70

ward was at least explained. After careful thought, Brian decided he must have had an accident, causing damage to his head which doctors had wrapped in bandages. Unable to remember anything since going to the BFI as usual the night before, Brian feared he must be badly hurt, and closed his eyes in an attempt to shut out feeling.

Impatient to learn what had happened, eyes still closed, Brian managed to push up the bandage covering his left ear and to listen in to the nurses' chatter as they went about their work. There had been an incident, apparently, in nearby Tavistock Square, a suicide bomber blowing up a bus, leaving dozens of injured, many of them being treated in the same ward with Brian.

There was always a reason. Misery of some sort. Or madness. Neglect, maybe. Politicians banged on about indoctrination but Brian saw the recent shootings and bombings around the world in terms more personal, public terrorism as a solution to private woe. Brian guessed there had been nothing unusual about the man on the bus with a knapsack on his back – he assumed it was a man – ordinary-looking, discreet.

It was all extremely confusing, as Brian was almost sure he was not in Bloomsbury that morning, a normal working day in the Camden office, and yet could not think of another explanation for finding himself in a ward full of the bomber's victims.

Relieved to have overheard the doctors confirm that he did not appear to have suffered any lasting damage from the nasty blow to his head, Brian decided to communicate, and asked the nearest nurse if there was a spare copy of the day's *Evening Standard* on the ward, in which he read details and saw, several times, photographs of what the paper described as a multiple terrorist strike at the heart of London.

In far-sighted preparation for just such an unthinkable situation as this, Brian carried with him everywhere in his soft leather bag all the necessary information, his National Health and Insurance numbers, contact details of his employer, next of kin, the name and address of his GP, together with his BFI membership and Visa cards, toothbrush, and a clean pair of underpants. In the mornings in the bag there would also be a copy of one or other daily broadsheet, irrelevant to the present accidental circumstances as the bag was missing.

Later in the day he had a visitor, Mr Wilson, his office manager, alerted by the police from the papers in the inside pocket of Brian's bag, recovered, he learnt, from the site of his accident. They had been colleagues for years, and Mr Wilson managed to convince Brian that in fact he had been knocked over by a motorcyclist on the zebra crossing on Camden Street, by the canal. Other patients in the ward had been injured by the morning's bus bomb, not him. Brian trusted Mr Wilson, though he knew nothing about the private man, had no idea where his boss lived, if he was married or not, their contact limited to coffee-chat about political sleaze, the football scores and occasional discussion of the latest box office success in the commercial cinema. Brian liked him, up to a point, and although he had imagined himself in Technicolor clarity lying beside the broken bus shown in the newspaper, he accepted that this had not happened to him, that he had movie-pictured the event in his head, accompanied by the overheard groans and cries of fellow patients. Mr Wilson moved the conversation on to a less emotive topic, the initiation at work of a new girl on the tea trolley, the arrival of which marked the twice-daily lightening of office spirits. She – Rosalba, by name – had bobbed chestnut hair, Brian learnt, and wore scarlet high-heeled shoes.

Sounded more Kensington than Camden, in Brian's view.

The girl's mother had emigrated from Sicily to Peckham before Rosalba was born, Wilson said. Brian had stopped listening, his thoughts elsewhere, on the kiss he happened to have seen a pretty girl in the office given by the post boy, pushing her against the shadow side of a tall green filing cabinet.

Or was it the girl who gave the boy a kiss?

Brian could not now quite remember, his mind muddled.

Lying back peacefully within a cradle of soft pillows that evening, the central lights of the ward turned low, Brian considered contacting his elder brother, his legal next of kin, in case he died. On discovering in the morning that his was not one of the names mentioned in the press he decided to stay silent and not, as he put it, upset the apple cart. Then promptly reminded himself that he had not been there anyway, and would obviously not have been named. Neither did he have the slightest desire to be in touch with brother Peter. Two days later Jack called by, looking drastically out of place in the sterile white ward, tiptoeing in his battered trainers gingerly across the polished green linoleum to the side of his friend's bed. Brian was thrilled to see him and to be filled in on the best of the movies he had missed. Jack had been totally taken, he said, by a documentary on the experimental rock group Einstürzende Neubauten and their leader Blixa Bargeld, ace manipulator of the jackhammer in motorway underpasses. Brian laughed in pleasure at the band's name and the titles of their songs, admitting that he had never heard of them before. At which Jack came out with one of those definitive phrases for which he was celebrated amongst his fellow buffs: 'After Einstürzende Neubauten everything is silence.'

The singer's actual name, Jack said, was Christian Emmerich, branding himself Blixa Bargeld when he left his parents' home in West Berlin to make music, *blixa* a make of blue felt-tip pen and bargeld a German street term for cash.

Before he left, Jack enquired about the state of his friend's battered head, asking him to take better care crossing roads in future. They wondered about meeting for supper one evening before a film, when Brian was out-and-about again. Invigorated by Jack's visit, Brian could not wait to get back to joining the regulars at the BFI.

He spent over a week in University College Hospital in Gower Street and was advised to take a further ten days off work before returning to his desk in the housing department. There were two things which worried him, considerably: the ugliness of a shaved patch above his right ear where the surgeon had placed fourteen stitches in his head wound; and the embarrassment of mis-imagining that at 9.40 a.m. on a Thursday morning in July he had been walking down Tavistock Square past the British Medical Association, a place which he had never heard of before.

Brian was horrified to read in the newspaper of the bomber's youth.

Hasib Hussain, aged eighteen, British born and raised.

What on earth had it got to do with him?

Why had he no recollection of a motorcycle knocking him down?

Things were wheeling out of control.

In danger of disintegration, Brian followed a tested path, pushed further examination of the episode into a locked recess of his mind and proceeded as best he could as if nothing much had happened. Which in ways was true, Brian decided some days later, smiling to himself at the rationalization. On his own the only things which mattered were those which he remembered and if he never thought about them, they, in effect, had not occurred. He found this concept universally rewarding.

The one thing he never wanted to do again was take a 168 double-decker bus home to Kentish Town from the South Bank stop on Waterloo Bridge, because its route passed through Tavistock Square. It was solely the Underground for him from now on.

Brian was more than ready to return to the rest of his routine, especially pleased to start back again at Il Castelletto for his daily lunch. Lorenzo was shocked to learn of Brian's accident, assuming he had been absent on a work assignment. Impressed by the naked scar, he refused to accept payment for Brian's meals for a whole week. Eating slowly Brian counted thirty-two chews every mouthful, hoping to quell his noisy indigestion.

At lunch on the Wednesday of his second week back at work, three of Lorenzo's musician friends called by on a break from sound tests for a gig that night at The Dublin Castle, around the corner in Parkway. The leader of the band, a nattily dressed dental technician called Massimo, was a regular at Il Castelletto, someone whom Brian always enjoyed listening in to, with his tales of tin-pot tours of the coastal resorts of Kent. Flyers for two of Massimo's past performances were pinned to the door leading to the toilets, with posters on the café's back wall for three or four concerts by bigger band names at nearby Dingwalls, the paper faded, curling at the edges. Another regular, Tony, whom Brian liked, an amateur DJ and self-employed plumber, joined in with the muso-gossip, the Italians mixing languages, moving on to swop plans for their holidays, the traditional long summer break soon due. Lorenzo was fixed to drive his wife and three children in Il Castelletto's unreliable van down to Umbria, to the town in which both were born and had received their first communion, where dozens of relatives still lived. Brian was perpetually perplexed by the density of Lorenzo's family life.

As Massimo left the café to return to his rehearsal, he clapped a large hand on Brian's shoulder at the table by the door and more-or-less ordered him to turn up on the coming Friday to a music evening at which he and Lorenzo were playing, in the pub at the end of the road in Bow where the Cerolis lived.

Reluctant to suspend his film ritual so soon after beginning again, Brian tried to explain that he was busy, at the cinema.

When the day came round and Brian noted that the programme at the BFI was riddled with romantic comedies, he decided to ditch his ticket and take an early evening tube train east, recognizing that Lorenzo was an important figure in his life and curious to hear him play his guitar on home ground. He arrived too early, with nobody in The Robin Hood whom he recognized – except Tony, preoccupied in setting up the sound system. So Brian went for a walk in the dark, passing what he guessed from Lorenzo's descriptions was his spick and span house, the smartest in his row, with a roof extension for the children, and then on around the adjacent streets, across a small park. Clouds hid the moon and it started to rain, wet cobbles shining in the lamplight, a sawn-off shotgun night in Brian's movie-imagining of the old East End. He was relieved to find Lorenzo and Massimo tuning their guitars when he returned to the pub. Shortly before they began to play Lorenzo's wife Francesca – Franny for short – pushed through the swing doors with their dog Eric, an overweight dachshund. Dog and woman were greeted with equal warmth by the landlord behind the bar. Brian had met Franny several times, when she used to help out at Il Castelletto, and he spoke to her with comparative ease. Lorenzo played modestly, perched on a stool at the back of the miniature stage, uncharacteristically wordless, leaving Massimo to front their gig, doing the introductions and making the jokes. The drummer was young and undeniably talented. Another man played adequate double bass.

It was a good evening. Brian was glad he went.

Even better was full resumption of nights at the BFI, notable in those initial returning weeks for two continental films, the first British screening of Michael Haneke's *Hidden*, passed on from the recent Cannes Film Festival, and an archive presentation of Chris Marker's rarefied linking of images in *Sans Soleil* from 1983. Brian could watch Haneke's female lead Juliette Binoche in anything, anytime, indefinitely. In *Hidden* he found Daniel Auteuil equally arresting, tortured by his guilty concealment of some unspoken act of the past, fearful – for reasons which Brian did not fully identify – of exposure and the subsequent collapse of his marriage and loss of everything he valued in life.

Straightforward on the surface but difficult to define, Brian commented afterwards to the gathered buffs. Mystery or allegory?

That's what was so good about Auteuil, one of the regulars responded. Communicated an avalanche of feeling. Never quite knew where you were with him.

Not meant to be a singular explanation, Jack said. Collective guilt. Retribution. Silence. Middle-class deceit. Racial exploitation. You name it. Haneke shoved it all in.

Brian had seen *Sans Soleil* before, for its sections set in Japan that explored rituals and practices of the Oriental past, whilst linking these to technological prospects for the future – as Marker himself said, Brian had noted: 'I bow to the economic miracle but want to show the neighbourhood celebrations.'

On the previous viewing it had not registered with Brian that Marker had involved in the sound production the electronic composer Isao Tomita, whose arrangements of music for the analogue synthesizer he had enjoyed hearing in several Japanese movies.

In the late summer of his return to regular viewing at the BFI, Brian sometimes arrived extra-early to sit and read the *Evening Standard* in a particular chair at a particular table close to the café's riverside exit. On warm evenings he sometimes wandered outside to shuffle along the lines of wooden trestle tables under the concrete arches of Waterloo Bridge, set out with inexpensive second-hand books. Later he watched the ordered way the dealers packed their stock into the black-painted chests lining the river wall, sloping lids triple padlocked. It was upsetting when the café altered policy and pushed out people like him to make way for paying customers, even when there were few people around needing his place. His stiff back tightened at the forced change to his routine, shooting spasms downwards into his guts, which dissolved only when he located a discreet row of comfy chairs back near the booking office, in which he could rest in spare moments. From this new spot he kept an eye on the electric clock on the wall above a board listing the day's movies, rising fifteen minutes before his film to make his way to the entrance of whichever cinema he had booked that night, to rendezvous with any arriving regulars.

At the end of the screenings on these fine nights, Brian sometimes chose to walk across the footbridge to Embankment Station, his gaze directed down river to St Paul's Cathedral and the glittering skyscrapers of the City beyond, averting his eyes from the commercial pretentiousness of the Charing Cross development. At isolated moments of anxiety, he had come to accept the fleeting sight of his elder brother around the station approaches, in response to which he crossed rapidly to the other side of the street, taking care not to look in the man's direction, fearful of catching his eye. Brian's evasive action was so swift that he never caught a clear enough view to be sure whom the danger-figure actually was, at different times wearing a baseball cap, a green mackintosh, a camel hair coat, once with a walking stick, shorter and taller, rounder and thinner than Peter used to be, as far as he could remember. Even face-to-face Brian suspected he might fail to identify his big brother, whom he had not seen since their mother's funeral in Rochester forty years earlier.

Peter had been based in Belfast at the time of her death. Maybe he lived these days somewhere on the Southeastern network, in Beckenham perhaps, or Bromley, and was on his commuter-way from a job in the City, home to wife and children via the mainline station.

Maybe none of the sightings were of Peter, still safely rooted in Northern Ireland.

Brian resented the idea that his brother might feel it his legitimate right to invade BFI territory.

Typical. Mean bugger. That twisted expression on his face, as if his teeth hurt.

Not that anyone in the family knew of his devotion to film, Brian reminded himself.

Peter's appearances were an illusion, a flash of fear, he

usually concluded.

Until the next apparition punctured this prudent resolution and, in a panic, he changed his mind.

Before changing it back again, resuming common sense. None of the men were Peter, Brian was mostly almost certain.

In his flight from all things Irish, Brian had developed a complimentary fondness for British cinema, a fistful of films never losing their capacity to entertain. One of the most vibrant was *The Entertainer* itself, he insisted to the other regulars after a screen revival, reading out loud a lengthy quote from the original *Times* review, reprinted in the programme notes:

> Sir Laurence, making the whites of his eyes gleam with a lost, mad emptiness, seeks to portray the agony of a soul conscious that it is moving within a set of circumstances with which it cannot come to terms... He may sometimes break the firm line of Mr Osborne's dialogue with a rocketing, fantastic and unforgettable display of broken and contrasting hopes, wishes, despairs, desires and resolutions, yet *THE ENTERTAINER*, with its capital letters, is a work of art, and the entertainer himself, humbly bereft of them, a man of courage.

Wow! someone exclaimed.

Did you see he painted a black gap between his front teeth, the white-haired buff in a suit noted. Clever touch, he added.

Interesting that both director and writer were bisexual, Jack pointed out. Richardson died of AIDS, Osborne from chronic diabetes.

One of the buffs muttered that, to his taste, Olivier was way over the top and Alan Bates, in his first film, stole the show.

Fancying himself as star-wary, Brian conceded this claim, whilst pointing out the awkward fact that, by now, Bates was himself a star, praised in the press for his final roll in Jewison's *The Statement*. A dead star, too famous to be seen as up-and-coming.

Brian held back from adding that he had always found Bates's modesty a pose, and suspected he had in fact been conceitedly smug, lazily content to play himself in every part.

Only sixty-nine when he died, of pancreatic cancer, Jack said.

The buffs collectively decided that Bates's acting pinnacle was in *An Englishman Abroad*, the BBC TV film about the spy Guy Burgess in exile in Moscow – a mix of Dundee and Glasgow in the film, to save money and evade Soviet censorship. Except for post-war Japanese cinema, the historical background with which he was familiar, Brian tended to experience film in the moment of watching, for what it meant to him right then, regardless of when it was made or set and how accurate in pretension it might or might not be. This open approach had allowed him to appreciate the quality of *An Englishman Abroad* despite his prejudice against Bates. It was much the same with those films he had seen twice, such as Lean's *Lawrence of Arabia*, Truffaut's *Les Quatre Cents Coups*, and the enticing Hanna Schygulla as Fassbinder's Maria Braun, which on each occasion he watched anew in a childlike kind-of innocence, amazed at different points in each viewing of the movie, seldom disappointed.

On his way home on the Underground after *The Entertainer*, going over in his head the regulars' wide-ranging conversation, checking that he had not made a fool of himself, Brian regretted not putting into coherent words to the others his objection to Coral Browne playing herself in *An Englishman Abroad*. A moot point, maybe, as she was excellent, and it was in fact her own story, based on a chance meeting with Burgess when she was touring Russia with a production of *Hamlet* in the late 1950s. Still a film, though, not history – Browne the actress playing herself as an actress opposite Alan Bates the actor playing a spy, with Glasgow City Chambers playing the British Embassy in Moscow.

Got that straight, anyway, Brian told himself with a sly smile in the direction of the tube map.

His smile broadened on unexpectedly recalling that Norman Jewison's *The Statement* featured a sheaf of first-rate British actors, including Michael Caine, Tilda Swinton, Frank Finlay and the ever-commanding Charlotte Rampling, all of whom acted Bates into the shadows, in Brian's biased view.

It was a relief on arriving home to retrieve, on a second search of the rubbish bin, his missing all-purpose kitchen knife. He had poked unsuccessfully around in the waste before leaving for the BFI and now that he had found it forgave himself for the stupidity of throwing the knife out with the potato peel.

In a wave of self-empathy Brian also forgave his mistaken visit ten days earlier to a fellow-buff, thick dark hair shielding his gaze, whose incoherent mumble made it difficult to understand exactly what he was saying. Regrettably, from Brian's perspective, the address the man wrote on a London Library ticket turned out to be in the red-brick block of well-to-do Edwardian apartments behind Westminster Cathedral. Furthermore, the travel diary which he had been invited to see was of no interest, inherited by the buff from his uncle, a British diplomat based in the Far East with a penchant for woodcuts, no mention of film, the Japanese material largely topographical, useless to Brian. The flat was crammed with stuff, barely room to move and nowhere to sit, hundreds of newspapers piled on the chairs and scavenged lengths of builders' timber stacked against the walls. A bright-eyed cat with three white paws hopped about the place chasing a yellow rubber ball. Already aware that the regulars were an incongruous bunch, Brian was annoyed with himself not to have picked up warning signs of this man's social background and disjointed state of mind. He left as soon as he politely could, hurried past the Catholic worshippers crossing the square and caught a bus three stops down Vauxhall Bridge Road to the Tate, to recharge his Turner batteries.

When Brian had first seen a picture postcard of *Rain, Steam and Speed* he had assumed, for several minutes, that he must be looking at an early film still, probably Russian. After reading on the back of the postcard about the Turner Collection, on his next free weekend he had made a visit to the Tate to see the real thing, and was astonished by the array of vast cinematic canvases by Joseph Mallord William Turner R.A., to name him in full. He had periodically made reverential visits ever since.

Things were definitely improving at work. Emboldened by the warmth of Mr Wilson's hospital visit, Brian allowed himself to voice openly his objections to the Camden office banter, which everyone else seemed to find amusing, laughing like donkeys. He was goaded on occasion into public self-defence, in particular against the term movie geek.

What did geek mean?

Nothing. An empty cliché.

He prepared in response the simple description of himself as a man who loved cinema.

No, not a film fanatic.

All he did, Brian said, was watch movies, causing no harm to anyone.

Fanatics assassinated heads of government.

Fanatics who were also heads of government invaded Iraq.

There was an aesthetic safety gap, Brian normally found, between film and reality. It was stimulating, therefore, to see how *The Atomic Cafe* broke with chilling glee the rules, a documentary formed entirely of clips from American cinema newsreels, television, army indoctrination films and civil defence videos. Brian was literally horrified by footage of the Alamagordo nuclear test site, swiftly followed by the clip from an interview with the US pilot describing the moment when he pressed the release button on the plutonium-explosion H-bomb above Nagasaki.

'That was the greatest thrill,' the man had said, grinning like an ape.

An even worse section in the film, for Brian, alienated in his Northern Irish childhood from the pious poison of religion, was President Harry Truman's remark to camera: 'God gave the bomb to us and not to our enemies, and we pray that He will guide us to use it for His ways and His purposes.'

Capital 'H' the optimum letter. For hydrogen, holy and hypocrisy.

The implications of *The Atomic Cafe* were beyond escape, leaving Brian visibly distressed, unable to join in with detached chat after screening of the film. He stood silent at the edge of the group, head bowed, unable to stem the flood of feeling.

He was aware that becoming a film buff had shifted his pitch of mind to the political left.

In theory, not practice.

Brian was totally passive when it came to political action, never bothering to place himself on the electoral register, not even after establishing a permanent address at the flat in Kentish Town.

While *The Atomic Cafe* had troubled Brian, British films by two of the fabled 'angry young men', Lindsay Anderson and Karel Reisz, had had a more sustained impact on his views of government, together with work by the next generation of socialist directors, Ken Loach and Mike Leigh. Certain European films had also impacted on his political thinking, most recently Michael Glawogger's *Workingman's Death*, premiered at the 2005 Venice Film Festival and shown nine months later at the BFI, a stomach-wrenching documentary about the exploitation of manual workers around the world. Glawogger's inventory on colour-rich film of the physical abuse of individuals and of the earth ranged from coal mining in the Ukraine, to Javanese sulphur hauliers, to market-stall butchers in Nigeria, to Pashtun ship breakers on the Arabian coast, to steelworkers in China.

At the buffs' chat after seeing this movie, Jack spoke eloquently about the film's avant garde score by John Zorn, recorded on the album *Filmworks XVI: Workingman's Death*, which the composer had issued on his own label, Tzadik Records. Jack owned a copy, he told them, which he frequently played.

A German film which influenced Brian's perception of politics, *Stammheim*, he had not seen on its release in 1986. Until watching the BFI's re-run he had known next to nothing about the Baader-Meinhof Group, with no idea that all five members were now dead, the first on hunger strike, followed by Ulrike Meinhof in solitary suicide before the trial, and then the other three, including Andreas

Baader, by co-ordinated self-death in Stammheim Prison on the northern outskirts of Stuttgart soon after being sentenced to life imprisonment. Brian was pleased for the opportunity to see this film, pivoting on a trial which had lasted for 192 days in the special courtroom built beside the prison. Sombre and fair, the dialogue in Reinhard Hauff's dramatized reconstruction was based on the actual texts and events. The BFI programme information reproduced part of the director's production notes, a section of which Brian copied down verbatim into the notebook he carried with him everywhere:

> The film documents a segment of the life and struggle of a group that wanted a revolution and that was denied any political motivation by the prosecuting authorities. It is a film about the inability on the part of the political realm and the machinery of justice to reflect the circumstances under which violence occurs; a film about the impatience and intolerance of those who wished to liberate the people, and who in the end merely brought about more restraints and even greater state repression than before.

Brian maintained that the political nature of Japanese cinema of the 1960s had remained strong and contemporary even when disguised behind historical narratives and costumes. A film like *Onibaba*, for example, directed by Kaneto Shindo, which Brian had only recently seen, seemed to him politicized and modern in its depiction of feminine strength and independence, despite the legendary setting. The two women at the heart of the film, a mother and her daughter-in-law who are obliged to fend for themselves by the absence of their men requisitioned by overlords to fight in feudal wars, learned with ruthless efficiency from their hides in the reeds to hurl spears at wandering samurai, strip the slain bodies of swords and armour and sell their loot for food. Stylized elements of gesture and speech, though archaic in origin, felt to Brian relevant to the emotions of today. And, whatever else, *Onibaba* remained enduringly beautiful to look at, not for the sake of it but in the landscape's intimate contribution to the narrative. The reeds of the marshes protected and participated, shown regularly at key intervals, filmed on each occasion low down and close to from the same angle, blowing in the wind, with an accompanying score of combined natural and man-made sounds, this abstract chorus increasing the drama. Brian loved the repeating stylized ritual. He read in one of his reference books a comment by Shindo:

> I aimed to capture the characters' immense energy for survival... I wanted to convey the lives of down-to-earth people who live like weeds... It is so easy to view social conflict with political idealism, or at least with tainted eyes, of political desire. I strive to avoid this by all means.

At one point in the film Brian was convinced that the fierce older woman had slain, knowingly, her returning husband and slung his body into the watery grave of her victims. He planned, in time, to check with Jack whether this was true, or his own twisted invention.

In the film-argument of exclusivity versus accessibility which rumbled inside his head, Brian took note of the number of popular box office successes he had seen at the BFI which were simultaneously a buff's delight, including Sergio Leone's *Once Upon a Time in America*. There were so many references to earlier movies in this film that when Brian saw it, he had extracted the notebook from his bag and made a list in the dark, in pencil, afraid he might not be able to decipher his writing later, hopeful that the mere recording of observations would help fix them in mind. He need not have worried, for every possible screen comparison was covered in the tidal wave of comments in the crowded buffs' gathering during the twenty-minute interval and then again on final release from NFT 1, with unrestrained rivalry for attention after concentration on this four-hour version of the movie. Brian's main offering was to pin-point scenes in the later movie in which the composer Ennio Morricone's plush sweeping score echoed more-or-less exactly, as far as he remembered, key incidents in *Once Upon a Time in the West* from sixteen years before. The violence of the massacre destroying Noodles's – sterling performance by Robert de Niro – family and friends shocked Brian, as did the screenplay's dismissive treatment of women, in caricature Italian fashion.

All-in-all, though, the pace and breadth of cinematic vision was quite something, Brian decided during his journey home on the tube. Deserved its status as a commercial hit.

Brian proclaimed the everyday element of his taste by also citing *2001* and *Alien*, far and away his top science fiction movies and the most widely admired films of their kind throughout the world, neither of which had he seen on their original release, contrary to the assumed practice of a bonafide buff. By now, though, he had seen both of them several times and analyzed the architecture of spaceships on film, wondering how such marvellous effects were dreamt up in the directors' heads in the first place, much less transposed technically to camera.

Who did not marvel at the daring in film of both Kubrick and Scott?

It was true, Brian admitted in his internal dialogue, that

he knew rather more than the average moviegoer about Japanese cinema, the product of his regular attendance at the BFI, a privilege not open to the majority, committed instead to family life and sport and booze and politics and the other things which people understandably chose to do rather than go out every night to the cinema. All the same, Brian was annoyed to detect resistance in England to Japanese culture in general not only to their films. Colleagues in the office were prone to use offensive slurs when grumbling about difficult Japanese tenants. When they made these insulting remarks, Brian bit his lip and stayed silent, with nothing to be gained by citing the sensitive and humane films of, say, Yasujirō Ozu, set in their present time, documents of measured reality. In his suppressed irritation, head down at his ratings desk, Brian's pallid face turned beetroot.

Building brick by brick in Brian's mind was the theory that Japanese cinema had developed its expressiveness in the late 1950s through being one of the few areas of life outside the control of the American occupiers of their country. Through film Japanese artists were free to register differences in visual and verbal language beyond the comprehension of General Douglas MacArthur, the Supreme Commander for the Allied Powers, and his CIA staff soaked in Hollywood movies. It was impossible for most foreigners to spot the subversion beneath the surface of outwardly serene movies such as Keisuke Kinoshita's *She was like a Wild Chrysanthemum*, made in 1955. Narrated by an older man returning after a long absence to the house in Nagano Prefecture where he grew up, the paired scenes at the beginning and end were of figures in a narrow rowing boat on a wide river, the composition based on Japanese woodcuts. Remembered episodes of the man's past appeared in filmed images within oval framing, each section introduced by recitation of a haiku, printed in English on the screen. The BFI noted that the director was influenced by René Clair and that four years before making this film he had journeyed to France to meet his moving picture idol. 'I really went to France so I could see Japan better,' Kinoshita was recorded as saying.

Brian loved the strangeness – to Western eyes – of this period of Japanese cinema, extending through to the late 1970s and films like *The Far Road* by Sachiko Hidari, one of only two leading women directors in Japan at the time, both of them having commenced their careers in film as star actresses. Hidari played the female lead in her own film, a practice Brian had his doubts about, recalling the uncharacteristic hesitations of François Truffaut's *The Green Room*, in which he directed himself as a guilt-ridden survivor of war. Regardless of the flaws, Brian nevertheless appreciated Truffaut's comment that self-casting had given him the same feeling in making this film as hand writing a letter.

Hidari had spoken of seeking to walk a convincing path between 'the image of a woman as seen by a man and as seen by a woman'. She also declared, according to a BFI note, that the many long shots in her films were driven more by sentiment than aesthetics, because 'when I cut, it feels as if the breath is cut short: the flow of emotions stops.'

Brian was heartened to read details such as these confirming that directors were as passionate about the making of films as he was about watching them. He trembled, as if travelling in the train itself, at Hidari's shot in *The Far Road* of a Titan steam train billowing smoke and emerging from the mist and rain, much like the Turner painting. And it had moved him to hear Nicolas Roeg say that he made films in order to feel less alone, matching precisely Brian's reason for seeing them, a comment of added significance by a man for whom Tokyo was his favourite city in the world.

It was possible through his research into Japanese cinema, Brian found, to seek solace on a wide scale when coming across the lectures and writings of the agriculturalist-philosopher Masanobu Fukuoka, heartened by the old man's belief in the need to accept insecurity, a life of flight more frightening than staying home to face the danger. It was right, Brian concluded, to resign himself to his limitations and not to try to run away.

In a fit of optimism he thought of inviting Jack to join him at the Barbican for a performance he had read about of the silent film *Safety Last!*, accompanied live by the Philharmonia Orchestra playing Carl Davis's new score, conducted by the composer. Except Brian was not entirely sure why he himself wished to go, as a good deal of pre-sound cinema bored him, indeed he found particularly tiresome the laboured stock-scene from *Safety Last!* of Harold Lloyd hanging from the hands of a Broadway clock. He had not heard any of Davis's music and suspected his preference might be, if at all, to watch silent films in silence, imagining a rouge-cheeked lady at a piano in the corner, rather than witness the caricature-of-a-man in black tailcoat and white bowtie flailing his arms at a symphony orchestra. And then there was Jack, whose company he enjoyed at the BFI but was at times embarrassed by in public. Brian winced on recalling the abandon with which his friend talked to strangers, engaging in elaborate conversation the couple in adjacent seats at their QEH concert and, on another occasion, discussing politics at length with a guard on the Underground as they had waited for a train.

In the end Brian chose not to go, and saved himself having to decide whether or not to invite Jack.

Brian saw himself as an awkward contrast in character between determined and vacillating. In his friendship with Jack, for example, he knew more or less what he wanted but feared the consequences, leaving him marooned in indecision.

In his private way he was organized and resolute. Never an actual boy scout, all the same Brian adhered to the motto *Be Prepared*. In a pocket at the back of his notebook he stored a contingency travel plan in case of emergencies, beside a folded tube map for instant response to unexpected interventions. The thought of missing an evening at the BFI frightened him, which was why he had rehearsed tactics to circumnavigate street demonstrations, striking train drivers, burst water mains, traffic light failure and any other potential hazard to the late afternoon cross-London traveller. Brian usually managed to anticipate the not-infrequent minor disruptions and take avoiding action without damage to his film schedule. Occasionally he found himself interminably stuck in a tunnel on the Underground system, with no escape. Whatever happened, as a matter of principle he always completed the journey to the BFI, even if the night's films were finished by the time he arrived.

In this, as in much else in his life, Brian felt comforted by sticking to trusted habits, benefiting from the stoic sense of independent self-discipline he had developed since the death of his mother. Some things were easier to handle on your own. Almost everything, in fact, in Brian's experience.

Steeped in film, Brian seldom had either the time or the inclination to switch on the small, rented television at home, the opposite of his pre-BFI nights when the set was seldom silent. He picked up enough of the day's news from listening to Radio 4 over breakfast and in his lunch hour at Il Castelletto from a thorough read of the newspaper, purchased on his way to work from the stall beneath the maroon-tiled arches of Kentish Town Underground. In an attempt one autumn morning at conversation with the paper-seller, a man who had wished him 'Good morning' every day for years, Brian glanced up at the Thameslink arrival board on the wall and asked where the over ground trains terminated - for something to say, not that he cared about the answer.

Useless, the man said, pulling a woolly hat further down over his ears. North to Luton Town but not to the airport. South to Sutton, with four golf clubs and nothing else. Suits a handful of commuters, not a scrap of use to the rest of us.

The newspaper man's language was more expressive than Brian's internal summary, the facts nevertheless clear. He was already engaged with other customers before Brian could think of a sensible response, turning instead to the barriers and down the escalators to the southbound platform.

On the way in to work, his thoughts switched to a new cause for concern, extra-worried about his lack of general knowledge, an unease subjected to several turns of the screw by the BFI's theme of the month, New Chinese Cinema. Courtesy of BBC radio and the *Daily Telegraph* Brian kept up to date with standard UK and US news and was adequately informed about European affairs, but seldom learnt anything of significance about the rest of the world and nothing at all on China. Desperate to fill at least some of the gaps before the regulars' post-screen meetings, Brian searched around for instructive facts. The new internet resources which everyone in the office went on about were patchy and anodyne on the Beijing film scene, he found, with a couple of asinine 'yellow peril' movie star stories and meaningless Peking Opera tittle-tattle. On the weekend before the season's opening at the South Bank, it was a relief to come across in Camden Market a dog-eared copy of an English language guide-cum-brochure to a film festival in Taiwan in the 1990s, which filled in some helpful background to Chinese cinema.

It was the BFI information sheet which confirmed to Brian that he was on the right track in his thinking, the transcript of an interview with Li Shaohong before a screening of her feature film *Bloody Morning*, which she herself had adapted in 1990 for the revived Beijing Film Studio from a published translation into Mandarin of the Gabriel García Márquez novel *Chronicle of a Death Foretold*. Born into the chaos of the Counter Revolution, Shaohong had received a minimal education before being conscripted direct into the army as an ignorant teenager. The death of paranoid old Mao had liberated the bright young woman to attend the Beijing Academy and eventually make this fêted film, in which she revealed the shocking poverty and oppression of village life in Northern China.

Now that he at least knew something of the world – tutored by film, by seeing it and then reading up in books about those movies which touched him – Brian recognized that for his entire pre-BFI life he had been a mouse, a termite, shut in dark tunnels of his own creation. Not that he had now become a lion, of course not. More of a squirrel. A marked improvement all the same. Opposed to the apportioning of blame, hostile to the concept of guilt, Brian had allowed himself to banish from accessible memory the boyhood years when repression and cruelty and the terrible incident of his youth had sent him burrowing underground for survival. Although it was no surprise to find that he knew so little about China, given his family's bigoted Unionist history, Brian was shocked to discover that his unquestioned assumptions – about the benign wisdom of Mao Zedong, for instance – were quite so stupidly, blindly, pathetically mistaken.

Inexcusably wrong.

How had he managed never before to have heard of the Long March and merciless death of tens of millions?

See no evil, hear no evil, speak no evil, in the words of Mizaru, Kikazaru, and Iwazaru, three very foolish Japanese monkeys, not wise at all, in Brian's judgement.

No way to behave, given the choice. Everyone, almost everyone, was capable of making the basic choices in how to act.

The principle of good behaviour had always mattered to Brian. Certain conduct he condemned as bad manners, thoughtless. Like being any more than a minute or two late for an appointment. Brian incessantly worried about failing to arrive on time, for anything, anywhere, and for safety's sake wore a watch on either wrist in case one went wrong – though the benefit, he admitted, was marginal as he had no means of knowing, if they differed, which of them was accurate. One of the few things which made him demonstrably angry was a latecomer to the cinema pushing by and blocking his view of crucial early shots of a movie. He had been known to refuse to get to his feet to let people pass and had twice written to the Chief Executive of the BFI to plead for the cinema's doors to be barred from entry once a film was in progress.

Don't be so strict, Jack used to say.

There was no such thing as forgiveness of sin, absolution the flawed indulgence of Catholics, Brian maintained.

Brian was as unforgiving of his own errors as he was of those by others. In spite of his cautionary planning, he was shocked by the inappropriateness of some of his decisions. Three months after an event in the spring he was still cursing himself for abandoning the BFI one night for a performance by the Japanese noise-maestro Akita Masami at the University of London Union. Since being introduced by Jack to the Einstürzende Neubauten documentary he had become peripherally obsessed with the related experimental sound in more recent Japanese as well as German movies. Masami, in the guise of his one-person band Merzbow, was the most imaginative of all the Tokyo musicians involved in esoteric film scores, and when on one of his Saturday-afternoon visits to explore the Senate House collection of film ephemera Brian had noticed the poster announcing a rare London appearance, he had immediately purchased a ticket from reception.

Already feeling awkward on the crowded stairway waiting for the doors to open, much the oldest member of the audience and the only person he could see wearing a tie, Brian was knocked back, physically, by the level of sound in Masami's electrifying performance on an array of laptops, home-made guitar, tape loops, distorted feedback, pedals, and shell baffles projected at incredible volume through stacks of speakers at either side of the student stage.

Bombed by sound, obliterated, Brian imagined Jack might have said.

A devout vegan, Masami dedicated one of his sets to an elephant seal in Ueno Zoo with whom he had made friends, incorporating the animal's recorded barks.

It was the bit Brian had liked best.

He did admire Masami's seriousness, his absolute concentration on the job at hand, stern-faced, black-clad from head to toe, long straight hair falling down his back, inwardly unconcerned about what others thought of his music, self-established as lone judge after thirty years dedicated to making his own noise.

All the same, Brian found it difficult to relate this performance to the Masami film scores he had heard. Disappointed by the experience, he vowed never again deliberately to miss a booked film at the BFI.

Such irresponsible behaviour threatened to undermine the foundations, he warned himself.

Keep watch. Stick to routine. Protect against surprise.

Normally Brian was able to anticipate passages in a film liable to resonate internally and was quick to save himself from hurtful effect. Almost all films affected him one way or another, usually, though, without consciously touching personal chords. Even inconsistent movies like Gregg Araki's *The Living End* moved him, with its portrayal of two young gay men in anger and destruction, their rash killing of a cop. The thing about the cinema, in Brian's experience, seated in a large dark space staring without interruption at a high wide screen, entranced, lost in another's vision, was that he found feelings inside himself he did not know existed, replaced the next night by a different film and new sensations. And the next. Another film, another set of feelings.

None of it was about him, all about the movie.

The unbroken concentration, the pure focus from beginning to end was what made live cinema such a wonderful experience.

Almost twenty years on from his initiation as a BFI regular, Brian still shook his head in disbelief at the pleasure of being able to see Mizoguchi one night, Naruse the next and Ichikawa on a third evening of the same week, as excited as ever by immersion in this other culture.

It had annoyed Brian when one of the other buffs, a sucker for rom-coms, had bracketed together 'that Japanese lot' in a dismissive sweep.

Not fair, worse than equating Nora Ephron with Hal Ashby, directors from different stylistic ends of the thoughtless regular's own cherished sphere of interest.

Ichikawa was seventeen years older than Oshima, the latter later making a colour film with multiple explicit scenes of sex. Performed not faked.

Ai no Korīda, it was called.

He should take a look, especially at the... No, wait, let him see for himself.

Might remove the smirk from his fat face, Brian had silently said of his fellow buff.

The English title *In the Realm of the Senses* bothered Brian. As the film itself had on the single occasion he had seen it, the intimacy too real and extenuated for comfort. He could not quite accept that the gruesome conclusion was based, as claimed by the critics, on an actual incident in the Tokyo suburbs. On the other hand, Brian held Oshima in total respect and believed him incapable of gratuitous porn. This despite the evidence of his own eyes, which he had found it necessary to cover from the sight of several scenes in the film, including close-up of the final inconceivable consensual act.

By then Brian had managed to catch David Bowie in *Merry Christmas Mr. Lawrence*, the Oshima movie with a gruesome botched ritual suicide, and was therefore prepared for physical challenge in his movies. Not to this extent, though.

As a matter of principle, in order to widen the angle of his film experience, Brian had made it his business to book in for other sexually provocative films as they appeared in the monthly guide.

With nil personal experience of the actions he watched, Brian's understanding of film as a medium nonetheless enabled him usually to tell whether what he saw was based on reality or invention. Until finding his feet in the genre, to Brian all of it had been almost unimaginable, and he was guided towards trust in the intrinsic value of what he saw on becoming aware of the commitment to this type of filmmaking by certain of the directors and actors. Serious intent was itself a quality, in Brian's mind, regardless of subject, a way of thinking influenced by reading an essay on a different subject by the director Lindsay Anderson, in which he argued that truth in film was an illusion and the only thing which mattered was the vitality of the work. In *Mano Destra*, for example, the director Cleo Übelmann was also the star of the film, a young Swiss dominatrix dressed in obligatory Nazi cap who tied up women clients in painful knots and photographed them, beautifully. Given the admirable energy and self-belief of the film, its different politics to Anderson's was beside the point. A cult S&M short, it was said. Although from Brian's personal point of view it was tame stuff by comparison with his discomfort in watching the mainstream sadomasochism of *The Night Porter*, Bogarde and Rampling at their arresting best.

Although Brian believed that he was never going to have sex, with anyone, ever, he was prepared privately to admit that, if he did, it could as easily be with a man as a woman. It would never happen, the idea of being alone naked in a room with somebody else too appalling to contemplate, of any gender.

To be without his clothes with another person?

Inconceivable.

If intercourse was forced on him on pain of death, group sex might be the least worst option. Seen from a progressive standpoint, the goings-on in Pasolini's S*alo* looked quite fun.

He assumed that Jack and the other buffs were much like him, basically celibate. Though he also wondered if one or two of them maybe visited prostitutes across the river in Soho on their way home from the BFI after the most stimulating movies.

Was there a sex fiend in their midst?

Several looked as though they could be, Brian discreetly acknowledged, amused by the idea.

Jack tipped him off about a provocative 1980s film titled *Clémentine Tango* by the French director Caroline Roboh, with its raw nightclub scenes set in Pigalle in which Roboh herself played the minor part of Blanche, a high-life socialite and clandestine stripper incestuously involved with her brother, one of the film's main protagonists. Jack told Brian the barely believable story that soon after she finished making this film, Roboh herself had married the Old Etonian heir to a Scottish baronetcy, smartly bore him two daughters and sued for divorce five years later in favour of a French sound-effects specialist, the father of her third child. A 'steamy shocker', Jack said the Edinburgh press had called her movie.

Brian planned to submit a request to the BFI to show *Clémentine Tango* in a future screening.

Where did Jack dig up all this stuff, Brian wondered.

Guarantee the baron and his sex goddess lived in a Highland castle, tabloid style, Brian speculated, his imagination alight.

A Serbian movie which Brian saw later that same spring, *W.R. - Mysteries of the Organism*, disturbed him not so much by the naked sex as in the director's free-wheeling from documentary to contemporary narrative to art performance to politics to psychology, set first in America and then Yugoslavia, where the film was shot on jarringly different stock. It made him dizzy, never knowing quite where he was. On reading the BFI notes afterwards Brian was irritated – without being sure quite why he was so annoyed - to find that the two lead actors had used their actual names in the script. The transvestite was a real person known in life as Jackie Curtis, and the woman filmed painting Sistine-cribbed canvases of female masturbation was the New York sexologist Betty Dodson.

People in movies were meant to act not be themselves. What was the point otherwise?

Once he had calmed down Brian realized that the director, Dušan Makavejev, had been playing tricks, that he intended these elements of the film to be annoying and contradictory, as reflected by his deliberately unpredictable cutting. Brian could not bring himself to admit that he fully liked the film, but on reflection did come to admire what he saw as its capacity for forcefulness without, however, needing to be dogmatic. Makavejev appeared to remain true to his own beliefs, true to his scepticism, and true to the power of film to surprise the audience into a new self-awareness. Towards the end of *W.R.*, the illusionistically-severed head of the star actress, still shouting abuse, dissolved into the smiling face of Dr Wilhelm Reich, defender and practitioner-in-chief of the genital orgasm.

Brian laughed loudly when Jack told him that Reich believed there was only one thing wrong with his neurotic patients, their lack of full and repeated sexual gratification!

When forced to think extra-hard about the movies he saw, Brian sometimes found his internal voice speaking in more complex words than he used out loud, or on the written pages of his notebook. He was unsure how this happened. It seemed most frequently to occur with work concerning gender and sexuality, issues evident also in some films ostensibly centred on conventional subjects, such as crime.

Like Clint Eastwood's *Tightrope*.

Such a shifting, subtle performance, clean cop Eastwood chasing filthy murderer Rolfe, with twists and turns in their contact with women until the two became morally indistinguishable.

Almost, not quite.

Eastwood's actual daughter Alison, twelve at the time, played his daughter in the movie. Real physical tenderness between them marked the difference.

As a matter of honour the buffs in their post-movie discussions seldom agreed with each other, keen to present an alternative point of view and to gift unexpected snippets of information. It was fun, anyway, to disagree, and gratifying to share with each other things little known. Aware of the importance to them all of watching movies, however ardent their disagreements they were never dismissive, always considerate.

Oddly, the BFI buffs experienced some of their most vociferous debates around Clint Eastwood, both as an actor and director, *Tightrope* no exception.

Which explained why the post-*Tightrope* gathering had been noisier than usual, everyone with an opinion. Jokingly, Brian proposed that Richard Tuggle, credited as both scriptwriter and director, was a pseudonym for Eastwood, and was vigorously corrected, as he knew he would be, already aware that Tuggle had written the screenplay of the earlier *Escape from Alcatraz*.

Starring Clint Eastwood, a chorus of voices observed.

102

That's how they met, someone added. Hardly a coincidence that the two teamed up again in *Tightrope*.

Brian faded to the sidelines, preferring in this instance to listen rather than speak, nursing some confusion of his own about a Hollywood movie which had dared in the early 1980s to expose the sexual ambivalence of its cop hero. Only half-hearing the discussion around him in the foyer, he was haunted by images of the pain he had noted on Eastwood's face, in expressive bewilderment at his character's unacceptable feelings. Brian was moved by the beauty of the actor's eyes, altering in colour between nearly blue and not quite brown above his upturned nose.

Jack made an interesting point about the guilt of difference and how the Eastwood character was initially distressed at lacking the butch instincts expected of a homicide detective and then equally shocked at his character's stereotypical male abuse of his wife.

It takes courage to be different, Jack concluded.

Easy enough once you make the break, someone said.

Wes Block, good name for a narrow-minded policeman, another buff commented, to the group's amusement.

It was this same droll regular – Ephraim, Brian discovered his name to be – who invited him to visit his flat in Stepney, to see if there was material in his library which he might like to buy, at the original cost years previously. London had become too arduous and expensive, too crowded, too big business for the older man's political taste, and he was moving to sheltered accommodation in Birchington-on-Sea. Rather than compromise with small screen home-viewing, Ephraim had decided to withdraw from cinema and during the twilight of his life catch up on the reams of Russian literature he had promised himself one day to read, written in his native language, which he had never lost during his years in the West. His hip was troublesome, he explained to Brian, but with decent eyesight for his age he envisaged himself happily settled in a comfy chair in the picture window of a communal sitting room, an open book on his knee and glass of Amontillado on the table at his side, the ocean visible in the distance. Brian wanted to ask about a group of framed family photos on the wall but did not like to pry. Before passing the contents of his flat to the relief fund for refugees run by his synagogue, Ephraim offered his fellow buff the pick of any film material that he might find useful. Brian's immediate eager acquisition was of an original poster for *Reservoir Dogs*, still in its protective tube, which he intended to frame behind glass and hang above his desk in the Camden Housing Office, Tarantino the ultimate film buff. If he had brought with him a larger holdall he could have purchased more, thrilled with the giveaway prices. It was nice, all the same, to buy twenty-three slim volumes of *The Golden Age of Postwar Japanese Movies*, published in the 1970s with bold figurative covers all by the same Tokyo artist, different but in uniform style – text in Japanese, masses of photographs with captions which Brian could not read, pleased to see that Ephraim had pencilled in film titles beside the images he recognized.

Ephraim's departure, one of the first to go amongst those buffs whom Brian had come to think of as almost-friends, saddened him. He felt set back on his heels, diminished by false illusions of permanence. It was a grave error to act as if nothing was ever going to change, and his getting things wrong in this way made Brian feel vulnerable. With film itself, in order to avoid repeated disappointment, he was learning to admire in anticipation only those movies he knew in advance, from past experience of the director's work, that he was likely to enjoy. In principle he habitually approached the viewing of film with eagerness but no specific expectation, thus able to come away with information of value even from work which turned out to be alien to his intrinsic taste. No filmmaker was ever completely written off, but over the years Brian had developed different categories of affection, in the top drawer of which resided a select number of directors – Werner Herzog, Yasujirō Ozu, Agnès Varda, Robert Bresson, Chantal Akerman, and Krzysztof Kieślowski, for example – whose work Brian liked watching regardless of subject. People who had already done enough wonderful things to deserve his loyalty. Every film they made had merit, he felt, even the occasional blunder. With them Brian might feel frustrated but never disillusioned.

Brian could not recall the quotation precisely, but he remembered agreeing strongly with a note he had taken down of Kieślowski talking about the lasting effect of film, just as much as all those things which actually happened, movies no different from real events apart from the fact that they were invented.

Familiarity with the body of a filmmaker's work cultivated a sense of companionship, so that when Brian spotted the director Jim Jarmusch make a cameo appearance as the film producer Monty in Rockwell's *In the Soup* it felt like greeting in the dark a friend across the heads of the audience.

He tended to select the month's films to see by topic as well as by director, to mix the menu. Brian felt too close to cinema itself and to the work of the individual people to operate in terms of good or bad, better or worse. All the lists and prizes, the Oscars and Emmys were publicity stunts, seat-selling, of marginal concern to buffs like Brian. 'Is it any good?' the man at the desk next to him in the Housing Department annoyingly asked when Brian happened to mention the name of a film he had recently seen, set on the Byker Estate in Newcastle. Brian never knew what to say in reply to this standard question, his focus on the character of the film, on its creative force and the nature of the actors' portrayals, not on a facile good/bad opinion. He had only brought the subject up because their whole department was busy at the time analyzing and comparing council estates around the country, including the Byker, a 1970s classic, location of the movie he had mentioned

One group of films which Brian allowed himself to look forward to seeing without fear of dismay was those with a cast of actors he admired.

Not just one favourite, nor two even, but several.

How could he possibly not enjoy *Viva la Vie* when it starred Charlotte Rampling, Michel Piccoli and Jean-Louis Trintignant?

Plus the singer Charles Aznavour in a character part.

And Anouk Aimée playing her beautiful self.

He had seen it the week before, with the full delight he had anticipated – apart from annoying programme notes, rare for the BFI, which quoted a pretentious speech by the director, Claude Lelouch:

> *Viva la Vie* epitomizes my deepest feelings, my credo. All my other films could have had the same title... The story of mankind is jeopardized because of dreams dreamt by some and taken over by others. There is only one step from a dream to an illusion. Only another from an illusion to a lie. And but another from a lie to a manipulation. In *Viva la Vie* one theme conceals another... Enough talk for now, let's make way for the film.

Much too much useless talk, Brian agreed!

As a bonus, in recognition of his taking minimum time off after the stay in hospital, Mr Wilson enrolled Brian on an all-expenses-paid public property seminar and study course in Leeds. Brian almost turned the offer down, dismayed at the thought of another enforced absence from the BFI, until persuaded in the end by promise of an astounding £30 a day expense allowance, irrespective of how much he actually spent. With his room and tuition paid for, and meals in the conference centre free to delegates, Brian envisaged saving nigh on £200, and advance-checked the Argos catalogue about upgrading his home PC.

Seminar. Delegate.

Brian the boring buff linked to classy words like that!

He looked forward to relaying this to Jack, and together laughing at the silliness.

Everything happened so quickly that Brian was on the train north before he had time to register quite how weird it all was. He ticked off on his fingers the novelties: number one, he had never been to Yorkshire; number two, never had his train ticket been paid for before; number three, this would be his first time inside a conference centre; number four, he now owned a desert-brown trenchcoat bought for the trip; and number five, not in his wildest dreams had he imagined receiving cash expenses of £30 a day. After a mile or two of anxiety at the strangeness, staring blankly through the carriage window at the neglected back gardens of Bethnal Green, Brian decided to try to have fun, and settled down to Derek Malcolm's *A Century of Film*, a reference book which he never tired of digging into.

The seminar itself was jargon-rich and information-meagre, but the site trips Brian found instructive, illustrating in the flesh the metropolitan borough's criteria for calibration of property types. Although Brian maintained his customary social distance, making no ongoing contacts, he did contribute to the field study discussions, the tutor thanking him for his intelligent comments. One benefit of his eleven days in Leeds, from Brian's personal point of view, was the Saturday afternoon that he spent in Holbeck, the mixed industrial and residential area in southwest central Leeds where Hasib Hussain, the bus bomber, had lived and gone to school. By now Brian fully accepted that briefly imagining himself in Tavistock Square had been a toxic aberration, not to be repeated, and this visit was triggered by his curiosity in the physical background to the one major event in which he had been peripherally involved, his memory undimmed of the awful injuries he had witnessed in hospital. He walked up and down the narrow rows of working men's terraces, many now occupied by British Pakistanis, wondering which might be the bomber's family's and what on earth they felt about their son's violent end. He skirted the red light district to catch the bus up to Leeds General Infirmary, where the mother worked as an interpreter for recent immigrants less fluent than her in English. Brian had wanted to meet Mrs. Hussain, to talk to her, though he knew he could not, should not, that it would be wrong to do so.

The organizers had arranged two short coach trips outside town, to Lotherton Hall at Abberford, run by Leeds Council, and to the National Museum of Photography Film & Television in Bradford. One of the lecturers had picked these sites to illustrate her critique of the commercialism forced on present-day cultural institutions, their expansionist practices devouring more and more money to make themselves larger and larger and less and less focused on the community's actual needs, visitor numbers and shop sales their major concern, allowing the quality of exhibitions to plummet. Presenting to the seminar's delegates a radical agenda, she argued that this kind of irresponsible action deserved the imposition of full rates and the withdrawal of charity tax exemptions. Brian admired the lecturer's principles without agreeing with all her solutions. At Lotherton Hall, an estate gifted to the City by the aristocratic Gascoigne family in 1968, they were shown a landscape architect's drawings of how the current enchanting bird sanctuary, created thirty years ago by an imaginative council officer utilizing Victorian greenhouses and the kitchen garden, was about to be torn down and replaced by Wildlife World, an undistinguished global-style zoo.

Paid for by us, Brian commented. In a hefty grant from the government of taxpayers' money.

A glutton for information, it did not always matter about what, inside the house Brian twice read the label on a smart suite of furniture in the main bedroom and wrote in his notebook:

> Supplied to Titus Salt Jnr. of Saltaire in 1865, in anticipation of his marriage the following year to Catherine Crossley, the carpet heiress from Halifax, made by Marsh & Jones of Leeds in solid sycamore inlaid with amboyna, purpleheart, alder and stained ash.

Brian sighed at yet another display of his ignorance, disappointed at being unable to tell which exotic wood was which.

The National Museum of Photography Film & Television, which had opened in 1983, was also in the process of transformation, into the National Science and Media

Museum, an altogether different animal. Brian assumed that The Pictureville, their spacious and costly internal cinema, was due for the chop, with the subsequent loss to researchers of the only venue in the whole world permanently equipped to screen Cinerama. He tiptoed away from the official tour to wallow in the simultaneous projection of three synchronized images onto a huge, curved screen. Few films had been shot in full Cinerama and the choice was limited, Brian happy to accept the show already running, *The Hallelujah Trail*, a pseudo-comic mockumentary with Burt Lancaster in the lead, a dire role which had set him back for some years on the road to eventual stardom.

On the short coach drive back to Leeds from Bradford, Brian sat beside a bright young surveyor, the only person on the course he had talked to regularly. She filled him in on what he had missed seeing in the rest of the museum and he told her about *The Hallelujah Trail*, striving to explain how he had enjoyed its awfulness.

Sounds a laugh, she said.

No, not funny at all. Dreadful racist stuff. Sexist. You name it. It was just that... well, in Cinerama it looked radiant.

They sat together again at the farewell dinner, delegates and teachers ranged at random down both sides of a single long table in the centre of the canteen, which was closed to normal service for the evening. The surveyor lived in Darlington, married with two small children. She spoke eloquently about her political commitment, aiming to run for election to the Council, in time, when her boys were a little older. Social services was the queen bee in her bonnet, she told Brian, incensed by negligent treatment of her dead mother. Brian revealed that his mother had also suffered from inadequacies in the system

– though she had not helped herself, he was surprised to hear himself say, what with drink and politics.

There were no speeches, no formal conclusion, people returning peacefully to their rooms to prepare for morning departures around the country.

On the return journey in the train to London, Brian wrestled with the contradictory facts that though in general he hated change, he was also incensed by particular things staying the same.

What could possibly be charitable in the status of private schools, for instance? And why call them 'public' when available exclusively to the rich?

In an anthropology documentary which Brian had seen at the last London Film Festival, where it won an award, a village leader was filmed explaining – in subtitles – that generations of men in their community had beaten their wives because it was the accepted tradition. Amongst other things, to encourage women to cook decently. It worked, the man in the film had said, patting his belly.

No doubt!

How unpleasant. one of the buffs had complained.

Mild compared with stuff on social media, another had said.

Because things had always been done in a certain way need not mean that they always must be, Brian had silently noted, disqualifying himself from public comment as he did not own a mobile phone

In the same breath, Brian was impatient to return to his own unchanged daily habits, eager the next evening to recommence his nightly viewings at the BFI. Maybe the key difference was between theory and practice – he liked the idea of change but for his personal well-being needed the days to stay the same.

Brian was excited to learn of the screening later in this first week back from the conference of Masaki Kobayashi's *The Human Condition*, in three parts, *No Greater Love*, *Road to Eternity* and *A Soldier's Prayer*, in original prints acquired from the National Film Centre in Tokyo.

They were long films, the first part almost three and a half hours, and watching them on consecutive evenings Brian experienced a euphoric re-initiation into the rites of cinema after his involuntary break. He was mesmerized from the first moment right through three nights later to the last, barely blinking frame by frame. Walking slowly over the bridge to Embankment after the final night, taken aback as usual by the size of the dome of St Paul's, Brian saw clearly why he was entranced by this period of Japanese movies. Everything about them – the style, the history, the language, the landscape, the story, the meaning, the emotion – was foreign to the British psyche. Unconstrained by the moorings of experience, the West watched the East without expectation. Brian sat stationary on a bench beside the northbound Northern Line platform at the Underground Station and let two Kentish Town trains pass by, numbed by a sense of loss at the end of the screenings. Sadness too at the movie death of the soldier Kaji, movingly played by Tatsuya Nakadai, with whom he had shared for hour after hour the epic injustice of war. The intimacy of film exhilarated and exhausted Brian in equal measure, left him slumped on the station bench, his back bent forward, slender hands resting on his knees, his bag pressed between his ankles.

The Human Condition, potent title – *Ningen no jōken* in Japanese.

He abruptly stood up, eager for a mug of tea in front of the electric fire in his flat. Plenty still to see, Brian assured himself, thinking of Abel Gance's *Napoléon,* an all-night affair, nine hours of silent mastery which he was determined to catch as soon as the opportunity arose.

If Brian could have had his own way with life, film would be his only concern. In reality, tedious logistical stuff intervened – such as the demise of his local launderette. After months of intermittent days of closure, the manager had taken the time to explain to him, with apologies, that she could no longer cope with keeping an eye on her barmy mother as well as looking after, on three afternoons a week, her daughter's baby and at the same time hold down her job at the launderette. One of them had to go, and with the other two she had no choice. After two days of panic during which Brian thought in his free moments of little else than laundry, on the spur of the moment he asked the advice of the newspaper man at Kentish Town Underground and was recommended the Washetaria down one of the side streets north of the station, in an area unfamiliar to him. It turned out fine, the walls painted in suds-like swirls of kaleidoscopic colour which he found a bit much, but the place was clean and warm, and customers habitually left the newspapers they had finished with on a shelf by the door, which Brian read as he waited for his wash – avidly if there happened to be a *Daily Mail*, too embarrassed to buy a copy for himself after a critical comment from Jack.

Brian's survival from the launderette disaster made the latest shock a little less bleak than it might otherwise have been: closure of the Royal Festival Hall for three months for urgent overhaul of the heating system, the café included.

Where to snack before the movies?

Something modest, as lunch at Il Castelletto remained his main weekday meal.

Somewhere to read the *Evening Standard*, brush his

teeth in the toilets, and take a catnap if time allowed, head resting sideways on his bag flat on the table to prevent theft. The RFH café was spacious and quiet, they were used to him and he to them. Not that he spoke to anyone, other than to comment to the cashier on the weather, or the latest exploits of the Royal Family. It was good, though, to be greeted with a silent smile of recognition by the middle-aged woman clearing the café tables, who had worked there for almost as long as he had been a customer. Vietnamese, he guessed, thinking of the street scenes in *Cyclo*. Brian felt comfortable in his regular place and was distressed to learn of the withdrawal of what he had come in modesty to expect.

Nobody was to blame, he knew that, and yet it did feel as if he personally was being unjustly punished.

On the next two early evenings Brian trudged up and down outside the other cafés and chain fooderies on the South Bank, and checked also in and around Waterloo Station and its railway arches for anywhere suitable. They were all too small and too loud, or too large and too alcoholic, no chance of fading away at 5.15 p.m. each day into a quiet corner with a pot of tea and lemon muffin. Out of the blue, walking down the pedestrian road between the BFI and the National Theatre Brian noticed through the NT's ground floor windows people sitting on upholstered banks drinking coffee. He checked his watches, saw that there was time to take a look before his film and walked round to the front entrance of the theatre, down inside beyond the Lyttleton bar to come upon a relaxed seating area and long counter serving reasonable-looking food and snacks.

The next night he went straight from work to the NT café.

And the next.

And the next.

Brian's pleasure at finding this new pre-movie refuge was tinged in bewilderment. For years he had looked on the café in the Royal Festival Hall as a vital necessity, a dependable element of his every day, until reality intervened to demonstrate that a nicer, warmer, comfier space existed around the corner, and had done so all this time while he refused to consider a possible alternative, any change in his routine a threat to stability.

Ridiculous!

More than just bewildering. Semi-deranged, convinced he was completely right when in fact totally wrong!

Doubly wrong, in his judgement of the RFH café itself and in believing that change was definitively disastrous.

What else should he be doing differently?

Brian stared through the plate glass casement out at the ranks of lighted windows in the tall office buildings on the far side of the Thames.

His frown softened.

Nothing different, was his answer. Essentially things were fine the way they were. Just good to know that change, if it had to happen, need not be quite as awful as he imagined.

Except prostate cancer, no mitigation there. Dennis Hopper had just died of it!

Film itself was the solution, tried and trusted, rescue in this case arriving in the indomitable shape of Werner Herzog and his guest appearance to top-and-tail an archive presentation of his early film *Even Dwarfs Started Small*. It was one of a negligible number of Herzog movies Brian had not already seen and at the screening in NFT 1 he enjoyed spotting aspects of this film which he recalled the director revisiting in a different form in later works, standard practice, he had noticed, for this most idiosyncratic of moviemakers – the dwarfs' tethered van motoring driverless round and round in a circle had been repeated in *Stroszek,* on the latter occasion billowing smoke and flames. If forced – by someone he cared for, Jack, say – to name a single favourite film it might well have been *Stroszek*, the screenplay sketched by Herzog in four days and then improvised on set by Bruno, his strange lead. Stripped down to bare bones, Brian saw himself as kith and kin to Bruno, institutionalized as a child and acting himself, a man who felt ignored and abandoned by the world after a brief period of praise for his roles in two Herzog films.

Bruno Schleinstein and Brian Saunders, capital BS twins!

Herzog, an exuberant storyteller, related to the full house in NFT 1 how at the end of shooting *Even Dwarfs Started Small*, in Lanzarote, he had racked his brains how best to communicate his special thanks to the cast of dwarfs, two of whom had been injured in filmed play around the circling van. As money-presents were not Herzog's style and knowing how fond they were of practical jokes he gathered them around the largest cactus in the vicinity and jumped into the middle of it from the top of a step-ladder. The onlookers laughed uproariously, Herzog informed the BFI audience – who also laughed loudly on hearing that it was months before the director had extracted the last cactus spines from his shins.

Herzog spoke at the BFI of the fallacy of literal truth in film, expressing ideas with which Brian was in total agreement. Reviewers had apparently seen the director's early films as largely symbolic, an error, he maintained, as these so-called symbols were simply things he happened to put in, more-or-less by chance, without knowing why. They seemed to be true, that was all, leaving him eager to discover what sense they might make by the time he reached the end of his film. Illustrating the point by describing a pair of feet sticking arbitrarily out of a wall in *Signs of Life,* Herzog said:

> They summed up what I felt about the place and its effect on the people. They were not literally true, and yet somehow they are true. At least, I feel that this is so.

Brian thought so too. It was because Herzog's integrity shone through everything he did, without needing factual endorsement of every single crazy idea. Such as walking cross country in a strict straight line from his home in Munich to visit the elderly film historian Lotte Eisner who was ill in a Paris hospital, willing her every step of the way to get better, for the sake of German cinema's survival, he dramatically asserted. By the time Herzog arrived she was back on her feet, confirming the success of his mission, he claimed.

At their gathering in the foyer after *Even Dwarfs Started Small,* a regular mentioned the film *Herzog Eats His Shoe,* by the documentary maker Les Blank, in which Herzog cooked and ate on camera the boot he was wearing after he had promised his partially-sighted friend Errol Morris that he would do so if he managed to complete an endlessly postponed movie project.

Trust Herzog to make a meal of it, Jack said, failing to suppress a giggle.

In the same week Brian attended a special BFI preview of the brand new *We Need to Talk About Kevin*, directed by Lynne Ramsay. His reason for going was not the film itself, as until then he had not heard either of its director or the novel on which the film was based, but to watch Tilda Swinton weave her celluloid spell. A dedicated fan of the BFI protégé Derek Jarman, Brian was grateful to him for his screen reveal of Swinton's pale face framed by long red hair, years before Siegel's *The Deep End* made her a Hollywood star.

The latter a tedious thriller, in Brian's opinion, in spite of Swinton.

Honestly, impaling a gay nightclub owner on an anchor!

Over his pre-film tea and biscuits at the NT, Brian recalled the warning by Jack, who had already read the paperback, to prepare to be shocked by *We Need to Talk About Kevin*, not in the horror movie sense, shocked psychologically. He promptly forgot Jack's comment as images from the previous evening of Herzog's grey grizzly-bear head took over and he speculated as to which, in principle, came first, his affection for the director or for the film. After an internal to-and-fro he ruled that for him everything always started in admiration of the movie itself, and that hearing the filmmaker speak was an enjoyable extra.

Memory of Jarman still brought to Brian's lips at unexpected times a smile. He remembered on a Q & A night at the BFI, the director's reply to the interviewer's suggestion that, being openly queer as a teenage boy in the Home Counties in the 1950s, he must have been made to feel a dreadful outsider.

Not at all. Everyone hung around our house. I was the centre of things, Jarman had said.

That's how he always was, to the end, Brian recalled, re-seeing his tallish figure in blue denims bounce around the BFI stage, eager for questions from the audience. Fleetingly, Brian regretted never asking Jarman, or anybody else, any of the many things he was curious to know about the directors of his favourite films.

No, it simply was not possible, the words would have stuck in his throat, stuttered to silence.

The embarrassment. In front of other buffs and all those people in the audience.

Swinton was a brilliant discovery of Jarman's. His death, though predicted movingly in his semi-documentary *The Garden*, shot at home in Dungeness and in which Swinton appeared as the Madonna, must have knocked her back. In four years, she had made five films with Jarman, based in Bankside with his close-knit gang of poets and actors and artists. In the last, *Edward II*, as Queen Isabella she had conjured a grand-guignol fusion of Margaret Thatcher, Grace Kelly, Eva Perón, and Mary Whitehouse. The effects of Jarman's illness from AIDS were undisguised by him from the public, his left eye half-closed, words torn, his much-loved humour and creative engagement as a result somehow larger than life. In *Blue*, premiered during his final months, over a bled screen of uninterrupted International Klein Blue the soundtrack described what it felt like to know you were dying.

After the screening of *We Need to Talk About Kevin*, Brian was able to assure Jack that, despite adoration of Swinton, he had barely been touched by the film and not remotely shocked.

Jack disagreed, for once, seeing the movie as a visceral display of unintended consequences.

Back at home with his mug of tea Brian realized that his failure to ask questions was more complicated than the physical fear of stuttering. It was partly because he never actually knew what he wanted to ask. On the rare occasions when he did make up his mind on what he wanted to say, he was afraid of the answer, and therefore remained silent.

When Brian arrived for lunch one day shortly before

Christmas, Lorenzo was in a rare temper, complaining about the Turks taking over the London café trade, under-cutting the Italians.

Must be rolling in it, Brian, he said. The money your lot make on business rates these days. Daylight robbery. Lovely cannelloni and salad for Brian, he added without drawing breath, shouted down the hand-cranked hatch to Dario in the basement kitchen.

How're you doing, mate? another café customer asked upbeat at the counter.

Same as yesterday. What's the difference?

To avoid catching Lorenzo's eye while he huffed and puffed around the place, Brian stared up as he ate at the familiar painting behind the counter, the idealized por-trait of an olive-skinned model with plunging neckline, competing with the muso-posters blu-tacked to the white tiles on the other walls of the café. The girl's name was Tina, favourite model of the late J.H. Lynch, a regular at Il Castelletto during the brothers' father's time. Brian had been startled to spot a similar Lynch painting at a screening of Kubrick's *A Clockwork Orange*, designated to represent droog taste in decor – whether meant to be modernist or naff, serious or tongue-in-cheek, it was hard to tell.

As usual Maid M – as Lorenzo liked to call Marian – was there, reading a new David Vann novel, her favourite writer because, as she had once told Brian, of the numb-ing cold of his landscapes. It was *Caribou Island* Brian remembered that she had been reading on the earlier day, from which she had quoted:

> She didn't trust the tricks of her own mind. Whatever she wanted to remember, she would begin to remember, until she wouldn't know what was real...

120

Cautionary words which Brian had never forgotten.

Lorenzo had calmed down by the time Brian had spooned up the last drop of custard and finished reading his daily newspaper. In the café lull post-lunch and pre-tea, Lorenzo admitted that the unchanging routine of running the café was beginning to exhaust his patience, he and Dario ceaselessly responsible for the place for over thirty years now.

Really? I need routine, Brian responded. One day is every day, for me.

They turned their conversation amiably towards a perennial topic, the satisfaction in being a fan respectively of music and movies.

Go for it, is my advice, Lorenzo said at the door, slipping out for a quick cigarette as Brian buttoned his coat and turned towards the Camden Council offices.

The other place where Brian could rely on a warm welcome was the barbers, a couple of streets away, where he had been having his haircut for years, every six weeks, the dates marked in advance in his diary. Joe worked alone in his small shop, men only, first come first served, no appointments, a twisting red and blue barley sugar sign hanging outside. A Turkish-Cypriot, the barber's name was in fact Yusuf, Joe adopted for simplicity's sake soon after he emigrated to Britain twenty years previously. Brian sometimes found the wait tiresome, forced to listen to the rabid comments of the client ahead, Joe clipping and tutting in response. Once he himself was in the adjustable chair, neck supported on the black leather roller rest, shoes flat on polished steel foot support, at the requisite angle, Brian felt as physically relaxed, he reckoned, as it was possible for him to be. Joe knew exactly what to do, the cut always the same – apart from mild modifications to allow in the passage of time for the scar above Brian's ear, his receding hairline and expansion of the bald patch at the back of his head. When Joe offered to 'tidy up those aerials', Brian agreed without knowing what the barber meant and was taken by surprise to find his eyebrows under scissor attack, and then pleased to see that their overdue trim made him look a little younger. Joe lived in Wembley Park, where he cultivated a productive allotment, and, like Lorenzo, complained to Brian about Camden's business rates. Regrettably, there was nothing Brian could do to help, he explained, as his job was to keep the freehold records up to date, playing no part in the fixing of bands.

In an attempt to make up for this negative response, from his shrouded seat in the barber's chair Brian launched into an incoherent description of a twenty-four-hour video, part of which he had seen the previous Saturday morning, of different film-clips of clocks spliced together to show on camera every successive minute of the day. Joe, he could tell, was pretending to listen, nodding his head from habit. Brian was not entirely sure why he was telling the story as he had regretted going, screened in a forbidding first floor gallery off Piccadilly. White Cube the place was called, the best new art dealers in London the *Evening Standard* claimed. There were not enough seats and Brian had had to stand, leaning against the wall, which must recently have been decorated, for it left a mark on the shoulder of his jacket. A pity because the idea behind the lengthy video was amusing, meticulously and exhaustingly executed, and he enjoyed keeping a tally of the number of movies he managed to identify. About a quarter of the clips during the fifty minutes he had watched.

New Year's Day was a special occasion for the buffs, the

day they had appointed for an annual gathering to submit and collectively judge their own private South Bank Award, at the one time of the year when the BFI was almost empty. They could spread out, give a short speech or two without fear of making a spectacle of themselves. The buffs had set the assignment for their annual award to nominate a notional addition to the defunct Museum of the Moving Image to rival its previous star attraction, the infamous dress worn by Marilyn Monroe as Sugar Kane Kowalczyk in *Some Like It Hot*. Ephraim had won one year with his proposal of the towering crescent helmet paraded by Minoru Chiaki playing the Banquo equivalent in *Throne of Blood*. Jack had triumphed another year, voted unanimously winner for the suggestion of Victoria Abril's golden pants from *La Muchacha de las Bragas de Oro*, the Vicente Aranda film. This year Brian was tempted to show off with some bizarre prop plucked from an esoteric source, but in the end held himself in check with the thought that what MOMI would have needed, if it still existed, was something universally recognizable to bring in the crowds, from one of the classics of the cinema.

What about that scene in *North by Northwest*, he deliberated, when Cary Grant flattened himself to the road to evade a clobbering from the single engine aeroplane.

The gift to MOMI of his grey tie, immaculate except for the archetypal Hitchcockian touch of a discreet dirt stain acquired diving to the ground in evasive action.

That would fit, he decided, with a neat story behind it for the caption, as before reinventing himself in the guise of Cary Grant, Hollywood man of the movies, Archibald Alec Leach was born and lived in Bristol. Local boy made good, perfect for a British film museum.

It was usually Jack, the senior buff, who marshalled their slips of paper, allocating a second vote if there was no clear winner in round one. This year he was able to declare Brian outright winner of their South Bank Award on the first ballot.

Brian beamed. Cheers! he said, and mimed drinking to the dregs a glass of champagne.

He considered wishing his friends a happy new year but decided not to, the meaninglessness of such ritual phrases an irritation, he found, especially at work, tossed around the office with hollow abandon.

Thank you. It means a lot to me. This is the first award I've ever won. Thank you, he repeated

Thanks too to the BFI, he added under his breath.

His alma mater.

If that was the correct term.

And even more thanks to key directors of film. People like Werner Herzog, whose book Brian was currently reading, published in paperback translation, *Conquest of the Useless: Reflections from the Making of Fitzcarraldo*. In amazement that Herzog felt such things, for weeks Brian had recited to anyone with the patience to listen:

> This morning I woke up to terror such as I have never experienced before: I was entirely stripped of feeling ...
> I was completely empty, without pain, without pleasure, without longing, without love, without warmth and friendship, without anger, without hate. Nothing, nothing was there anymore, leaving me like a suit of armour with no knight inside.

As retirement approached, whether he had a genetic weakness of the spine or due to decades of his stooped working posture, Brian had by now acquired a distinct hump near the top of his back, stretching his jacket and making him bend slightly as he walked, neck angled forward like a

124

harmless vulture. In three months he was due for retirement and planned, with an inner smile, to do so without telling any of his colleagues, keen on the surreptitious idea of simply not turning up on the day in question in the unverifiable hope that they might not immediately register his absence and carry on as if seeing him there at his desk as usual, the ghost of nothing. Unverifiable because Brian had no desire to meet up again with anybody from the office and would therefore never know what happened on the morning after he left.

With the exception of Mr Wilson, who knew that he was leaving and with whom he had some time ago exchanged telephone numbers. As a precaution, not expecting to need to be in contact.

Brian had mixed feelings about stopping work. On the one hand, after two substantial changes in office record keeping during his working life, he was pleased not to be around for the third, a full digital revolution. On the other hand, he was anxious about how to occupy the empty days ahead. He felt uncertain in almost everything, always had, the sense of insecurity which this bred a significant reason for the muted life-choices he had made. During the three months left at Camden's Housing Office Brian spent a good deal of time staring up at the Tarantino poster hanging above his desk, to solicit inspiration from Mr Brown, Mr Blue, Mr Orange and Mr Pink as he racked his brains how to usefully fill the free time which was about to become his. His poster had made a brief appearance in the documentary *Property of the Council,* shot in the Camden offices by Channel 4 the previous year. Several of the girls from the floor below – Pools and Playgrounds, as the department was known – were interviewed on camera, dressed up for the occasion in tight pencil skirts and dense mascara. Two of his colleagues in Housing also briefly appeared in the film. Brian had not been approached by the filmmakers, to his relief.

He had written a postcard to Ephraim in Birchington-on-Sea to tell him about his poster in the TV film and was disappointed not to have received a response.

Was it Mr Orange, the undercover agent, whom Brian imagined he heard suggest that to learn a language would be profitable use of his spare time?

He raised an eyebrow to the poster at the idea. Honestly, he was perfectly happy with subtitles, certainly preferable to seldom-synchronized translation.

Sleep in and breakfast at leisure, Mr Pink might have proposed, rejected by Brian as, in his case, unlikely.

He could always catalogue his film books and brochures, amounting by now to what others might claim to be a library. To say nothing of the thousands of A4 film sheets packed on both sides with information, retained by Brian from every single screening at the BFI he had ever attended, tidily stored in ring-binder files – in date order of viewing, charting a chronological history of his developing taste in cinema. These needed listing alphabetically by director and lead actors, cross-referenced by title and release date and, ideally, indexed with a two-sentence summary of each movie's plot. He could stretch out this task for at least a year, as far perhaps as his sixty-seventh birthday. Longer if he used the sheets as base-guide to record for the BFI Research Library a comprehensive reference tape on the Japanese film studios, sharing knowledge and ideas formed over his years of enthralled looking and annotated research. Then there were the shoe boxes of early postcards of cinemas, they needed cataloguing too.

That still left at least a decade to go, maybe longer, as his father had lived to be eighty-two. Since his departure as a boy Brian had not once visited Northern Ireland, even for the old man's funeral. It was one decision Brian never questioned, never regretted, his father's action all those years ago beyond forgiveness.

In his retirement deliberations Brian recognized that if he were to make a wrong move now at this delicate stage there was the danger of his facing 'an abyss of nothingness' – in the words of Bergman, a director he revered, memorizing several of his sayings.

Brian's overall anxiety led him to give serious consideration at one point during his final fortnight of work on the Borough's rates to applying for another job, maybe filing clerk in a solicitor's office, or volunteer in a charity shop – with the standard state pension plus public sector top-up he had money enough to cover his modest living expenses and did not need to be paid. For a mad moment Brian thought of asking Mr Wilson if he could stay on at his desk in Camden for a trouble-free year or two and thus avoid having to ask for help to transport back to his flat the large framed Tarantino – a rare original poster from the slated debut screening of *Reservoir Dogs* at the Sundance Festival in January 1992, he had told Mr Wilson when asked, giving a detailed answer for once to the benign manager, in a goodwill gesture on imminent departure.

He knew that his thoughts were in a mess and suspected that he needed help to straighten things out in his head. At a previous time of debilitating indecision Brian had spoken to his GP, a sympathetic Jamaican woman who had listened attentively to his story and made a longer appointment to see him again later the same week. At the end of this second talk the doctor had advised that, regrettably, there was little she could do for him as the psychotherapy he needed was unavailable these days on the National Health and the current fashion for recourse to SSRIs was inappropriate, in his case, indeed for most of the patients erroneously given the 'magic' pills, she added.

Papering over the cracks. To save face and money, she had said.

He was on his own, in effect, Brian had concluded.

One useful strategy she had suggested was for him to avoid situations and individuals he found difficult and thus reduce the strain. There was no shame in self-protection, his GP had said. Quite the opposite. Most people deserved to treat themselves much better than they did.

Recalling what the doctor had advised on the earlier occasion, Brian managed to calm down and clip his retirement panic. At heart he knew how important it was to keep up the effort to escape his demons. He also knew that he never could, that the rescue ladder would always break and hurl him back into the pit.

The source of this evocative image came from a film he had just seen, for the third time in twenty-five years of attendance at the BFI, *Woman of the Dunes*, directed by Hiroshi Teshigahara in 1964 from a screenplay by the poet and novelist Kōbō Abe. Brian felt less certain now about what precisely he was seeing than he had been at first sight all those years ago. An extraordinary film, in which he found only sporadic narrative or emotional clarity whilst it nevertheless commanded his attention from start to finish, of a man trapped indefinitely at the bottom of deep hole in the sand, with a woman who had already built for herself a wooden shelter in a side tunnel, to give the modicum of privacy from inquisitive neighbours poking their heads over the rim. There were moments in the film when Brian suspected that the woman did not, in fact, exist and was a figment of the man's composite memory of sexual encounters in his life beyond entrapment in the dunes.

The man was an entomologist working on field-research into the insects of the sands, Teshigahara helpfully informed the viewer early on in his film, information which it was easy to forget, sidetracked by many urgent diversions, such as the quest for drinking water, official visits from the village elders silhouetted against the sky above, a burning cloth on a pole, the repeated shovelling of ceaseless waves of falling sand, and the woman's miscarriage.

At one point an unseen hand lowered a long wooden ladder down into the pit, the rungs of which broke as the man made a frantic dash to climb free, landing him back in oblivion.

Select sections of the Takemitsu score sounded electronic, the notes withdrawn before fully heard, Brian commented to Jack in the foyer.

A chamber ensemble, Jack responded. Those string drones, extraordinary.

Brian did not tell his friend, or anybody else, about a disturbing incident that had occurred soon after eleven on the Thursday night of the week before, when he was stopped by the police as he walked home down Kentish Town Road from the tube station. An unmarked car had screeched to a halt and three plainclothes officers had jumped out, two of them pinning him to the bonnet and the third unzipping his slim leather bag and emptying its contents onto the vehicle's roof. He was instantly released and the police apologized, genuinely Brian felt, explaining that they had been informed on their shortwave radio half an hour earlier of a man matching his description who had nicked a woman's handbag at The Lion and Unicorn in nearby Galsford Street.

Not you, the shorter of the officers had said. Innocent, obviously.

Brian did not feel innocent.

How could he?

Everything he touched went up in smoke, always had, since childhood. He was a disaster zone. However hard he tried to stay secure he never managed to for long, assailed by a string of failures for which he alone was blamed.

In Brian's view his relationship with film was the sole exception, underlining the value of his human contact with fellow buffs at the BFI. Riddled with doubt, he needed to tell himself this over and over again.

Inner disquiet made him unobservant of things around him, distracted by the noise in his head, and it was ages before Brian registered that the talkative group on whom he used to spy had stopped coming even occasionally to the BFI, and some time later before he became properly aware of the sporadic attendance of highly specialist bands of fans to certain cult movies. The loudest were *The Rocky Horror Picture Show* lot, several of the men in Tim Curry wigs. Once he had noticed another group, The Get Carter Club as he christened them, Brian became quite attached to the double row of youngish men who appeared whenever early Michael Caine movies were screened, chatting eagerly in exaggerated South London accents. Not until his second viewing of *Get Carter* did it click with Brian that the gangland boss who paid for Jack Carter's assassination on the banks of the Tyne in the final shots of the movie was played by John Osborne, screenwriter of *The Entertainer*. The long-range bullet hit the precise centre of Caine's forehead, making a neat red hole in his city-pale skin. Several members of the notional club wore Union Jack waistcoats to their ritual viewings.

On the outer ring of the small solid core of BFI regulars, peripheral figures came and went – Brian seldom knew exactly why, usually due to relocation for work, he presumed. He was a poor judge of which of the newcomers would stay the course and had not expected a modest Indian man to become the regular he had now been for several years, providing language assistance to Jack in his never-quite-complete research into pre-1960 Bengali cinema.

Jack said the buff was a solicitor, like Gandhi, at a small commercial practice in Ealing. A Hindu, also like Gandhi.

Brian's knowledge of the Mahatma was limited to Attenborough's film, of which he had been uncharacteristically dismissive, rejecting it as romanticized white-wash, a verdict with which Jack concurred.

Pranshu was born and brought up in Uganda, Jack explained. Until Idi Amin went on the rampage and the family was resettled in Portsmouth, where he and his sisters went to secondary school.

Brian knew so little about other people because, unlike Jack, he never asked, forever evading the personal.

It was upsetting to find mention of India turning his thoughts again towards the Pakistani boy and his bomb on the bus. Keen to witness the scene of mayhem, with the hope of somehow quietening the memory in his head of hospital cries, Brian returned occasionally to Bloomsbury. He had combined his recent trawl of the area with a visit to the show of Shunga erotic woodcuts at the British Museum. Exiting at the back to face the towering University buildings, for a moment he wondered if his reason for being there may have been some film stuff he had needed to research in the Senate House Library.

Ridiculous!

No, no, he was hit by a motorcycle in Camden Street

on his way to work.

Get real, he told himself, repeating something some-one had said in a film.

The Japanese prints were too genital for Brian's taste. Technically brilliant, the detail embarrassing to expose in public, Brian found. Although there was no-one in the gallery whom he knew, it felt awkward to be caught looking at them.

The night before the accident he had seen Jim Jarmusch's *Broken Flowers* at the BFI and although he could not now remember a single specific scene in this low-key movie, he retained what he felt was the clear recollection of arriving home afterwards.

And then... blank.

Until coming round with his head resting on the curb. This he definitely remembered, without at the time knowing were he was..

A stranger had cradled his bleeding head in her lap and held his hand, an act of tenderness beyond Brian's comprehension.

The driver of the motorcycle had not stopped and was never found.

Brian tried to work out what he had done wrong to get knocked over on a pedestrian crossing, anxious to make sure it did not happen again.

Thoughts jumped around out of control, shocks of the past invading the present. Tense and perplexed, the current prospect of retirement's disruption of his life-routine affected every aspect of his day and night. At a time like this of invasive stress, Brian's mind inevitably returned to dwell yet again on this moment of drama.

When seeking advice from the regulars about retirement Brian tended to invite them in turns to join him for coffee on the riverfront as the group dispersed post-film.

The contradictory suggestions he initially found confusing, until having time on the twenty-minute tube journey home to Kentish Town to think about their counsel. He liked best the idea of applying for an usher's vacancy at the BFI, although he feared he was probably too old to be considered for the job. Too decrepit, not up to all the standing around at the cinema doors.

Someone said he might like to re-train as a snooker referee.

Brian laughed, aware that the man was joking, typical buffs' repartee in reaction to the restored print they had just seen of *The Hustler*, with Paul Newman as Fast Eddie, a gullible pool player. In their after-screen chat one of the regulars had questioned Newman's physical suitability for the role and another, in principle a fan of the actor, had nonetheless agreed that he was better suited to hero than loser.

What about *Butch Cassidy and the Sundance Kid*, victor or vanquished, Brian wondered.

Largely in response to worry, he guessed, Brian developed the kind of acute earache he used to suffer from as a boy, and decided to consult his GP, still the same considerate woman. After examination with an otoscope, she informed him that there was nothing seriously wrong. She prescribed a solution of warm water, baby oil and diluted hydrogen peroxide dripped into the sore lobe at night for a week, and to stop poking around with cotton buds as it was obvious he had been doing – indeed never to put anything smaller than his elbow into either ear, she admonished, shaking a finger at him.

The blunt end of a pencil, actually. He had never touched a cotton bud in his life and was not at all sure to what use they were meant to be put.

Brian felt immediately better after seeing the doctor,

and three days later the pain vanished, without his needing to follow her prescription.

Unable to make up his mind which of several alternative plans to follow, Brian dithered, let decisions slip and in the days immediately after retiring from work at the Housing Office found himself watching two films every evening at the BFI, seven days a week, and in the mornings working in his flat slowly through his books, brochures, and leaflets, ordering and cataloguing and noting down thoughts and quotes to return to later. His one initial divergence was a fortnightly visit to the three second-hand bookshops in London which years of experience had taught him were the places most likely to stock film material of interest, one in Charing Cross Road, another on Upper Street in Islington and the third his old favourite off Ladbroke Grove. Now he had retired, Brian found the time also keep a consistent watch on the stalls in Camden Market, where rare cinema magazines and movie ephemera occasionally surfaced. He bought carefully, unable to afford the recognized classics, exploring instead the hidden byways of Japanese cinema – secondary sources, mostly photographic. He liked the spoken sound of Japanese, and indeed the shapes of the word diagrams, and vaguely wondered about learning the language, but did nothing about it. Brian's routine was periodically interrupted by a week of daytime visits to the BFI Research Library, steadily inspecting the many books missing from his amateur shelves at home and – especially – mining their extensive collection of Japanese video recordings.

A phrase had lodged in his mind from seeing in one of the library's viewing booths Shigeko Kubota's *Meta-Marcel*: 'It snows in my video window as it snows in my mind.'

He was building up the courage to watch without flinching her short film *Vagina Painting*, from a notorious performance at the Perpetual Fluxus Festival in New York in 1965.

Aware of the increasing prevalence of the moving image as a form of expression in the visual arts, Brian had begun to keep regular look-out for relevant video work shown in London's public and commercial spaces. Wherever possible he avoided the West End, intimidated and offended by the cool reserve of swank galleries, his feeling of alienation so strong that at times he sensed an unseeable physical barrier preventing his entry. All the same, if there was something showing which he really wanted to watch, he went – in this instance to a video exhibition by one of the doyens of the field, Bill Viola, at a Bond Street art gallery.

The work of Viola's in the show which Brian particularly wanted to see was titled *The Quintet of the Unseen*, in which five actors in contemporary dress, three women and two men, were positioned in a close-knit group, the form modelled on early Renaissance paintings. Filmed against plain grey and looking out as if at some dramatic unseen action beyond the camera – a crucifixion, the beheading of St Cecilia? – the actors expressed extreme emotion, captured in little more than sixty seconds of film which Viola had ultra-slowed down to sixteen minutes projection for his video. Small movements of hand and arm, the opening and closing of a mouth, the excruciating alteration of expression in the eyes from joy to agony, were felt by Brian with extra weight experienced at the pace of a snail.

The videomaker was quoted in the gallery's press release:

Our work today as artists is not about describing the arrival at or possession of a goal, but instead it is about illuminating the pathway. It is not about a system of proofs and declarations, but a process of Being and Becoming.

Tosh!

Neo-Nietzschean cliché.

The sad self-importance of an overpraised artist with an irritating Shakespearian surname.

Mainstream filmmakers too were guilty of pomposity, Brian admitted. Less so, though, in his view. And with greater weight of personal commitment, given the length of time it took to realize a feature film and the hordes of people involved in the making.

The Viola piece reminded Brian of a work by Gillian Wearing, from a retrospective of her videos he had seen at the BFI. Like *The Quintet of the Unseen*, her *Sixty Minutes Silence* also relied on patient viewing, of three rows of uniformed male and female police posed for a formal group photograph, initially appearing to be a still image, until small movements caught the eye, the twitch of a nose, the adjustment of an earring, a throat sweet popped into the mouth by a seated senior officer. Brian had gazed at the video with growing apprehension, convinced that something bad was going to happen. Close to the end of the hour, one of the twenty-six actors dressed up as the police screamed, the first – and last – sound in the piece. This blast of frustration made Brian jump, and then laugh at the appropriateness.

He liked Wearing a whole lot better than Viola, that was clear.

A bias towards British filmmaking over American?

Probably, he allowed.

At least the smart premises opened when they said

they would, unlike a basement gallery on Chapel Market which Brian visited on the same day as the Viola, hoping to see a new video by the talented Ben Rivers, to find it inexplicably locked shut.

Some filmmakers were also painters, graduates from art not film school, making objects as well as moving images and, in Derek Jarman's case, a wayward garden on the pebbles of Dungeness. It did not seem to matter which came first, pictures or film, a single creative spirit was engaged. Brian was keen on seeing the lesser-known early work of the multi-disciplined directors he admired, to gather some sense of the process of how they found their voice in the medium of film. He was excited, therefore, at the chance to see in the BFI Studio two of Jarman's Super 8 movies of the early 1970s, *Journey to Avebury*, with electronic score added in 1996, two years after the artist's death, and *My Very Beautiful Movie (Fire Island)*, six minutes of beach joy on Long Island, New York.

In the discussion afterwards, Brian was surprised to note that few of the buffs attending had seen any of Jarman's early work before – even Jack was relatively uninformed, though he appreciated the soft focus and filter-warmed colours of the Wiltshire lanes and fields in the Avebury film

Like a John Nash watercolour, Jack said. The neglected brother.

Brian filled in his fellow regulars on Fire Island, a semi-private club and resort favoured by the gay art set, where Hockney used to stay when he was over in New York from his home at the time in California.

Maybe that's where Jarman caught AIDS, someone suggested.

More likely Hampstead Heath, the bicycling buff corrected. Derek so loved the Heath.

Brian disliked this type of uninformed gossip and regretted saying anything about Fire Island, his remarks meant to be informative rather than salacious. Although Jarman would not have been in the least bothered, so open and relaxed, he reminded himself.

In the same series of screenings at the BFI, Brian saw a curious sixty-minute video by the designer of Jarman's sets and costumes for *Jubilee*, the engagingly radical John Maybury with his *Promotion of Absurd Perversion in Sexual Personae Part I*, a collage of images gathered over many years in London's punk and gay worlds, a multiform mixing of sound and pictures. Brian was simultaneously both confused and amused, uncertain quite what to write in his cumulative notes about film directors and sex, Maybury's language and experiences foreign to him.

One of his problems was that when actors were lying face down naked, or seen in close-up from behind standing without clothes, Brian found it hard to tell for certain male from female bottoms. In a flash of mad speculation during the Maybury screening he was distracted by wondering if his favourite arse on film, Vogler's in *Kings of the Road*, might have been a woman's, cast for her filmic round white cheeks.

Despite being somewhat of a connoisseur of cinema nudity, he lacked live experience and, given a cameraman's tricks of the trade, could not be sure which was which, nevertheless suspecting that female buttocks tended to be fuller than male.

Could easily have been a stuntwoman shitting in the dusty grass.

The screen shots playing inside Brian's head switched to another Vogler role, Philip in Wenders's *Alice in the Cities*, a disillusioned young writer who felt obliged to help an abandoned ten-year-old girl locate her grandmother's distant home. In Brian's memory of the film the girl, Alice, preferred the Vogler character and his attitudes to life to anyone in her own family, too busy being rich to take more than perfunctory notice of her feelings. It was as if, Brian felt, she had decided early on, as a really young child, that the grown-ups around her house could not be relied upon and she had best learn to look after herself. With the result that Alice was more at home in the world in some ways than Philip.

More than Brian himself that was for sure.

Women, he suspected, were genetically sharper than men – true of the only woman he knew at all well, Marian, his occasional lunch companion at Il Castelletto.

On his way home in the tube from the Jarman shorts he broke into a broad smile, remembering something Jack had said about David Hockney reading in his local Yorkshire newspaper the headline 'Two Boys Cling to Cliff All Night', assuming it referred to his favourite pop singer Cliff Richard and thinking lucky boys!

Hockney put the quote in one of his paintings, Jack said.

Brian looked it up, surprised to find that *We Two Boys Together Clinging* was painted during Hockney's second year at the Royal College of Art, aged twenty-four, not long down from Bradford. Brian loved to see prodigious talent in early works, by visual artists as well as by film-makers. Sad when promise was later dissipated.

Back at another week of research in the BFI library, Brian was rewarded one morning with the invitation from a senior curator to contribute any information he might be able to excavate over the next month on *Tokyo Story*, for a gala screening. The Ozu film, though completed in 1953, had not been released in the West until 1972, nine years after the director's death, and then only in a poor internegative struck from positive prints, the original destroyed by a fire in the laboratory. A year ago, the director's own copy had come to light in the possession of distant heirs of Ozu's in Kyoto and it was a borrowed print from this which the BFI had scheduled. With the help of the cultural attaché in the Japanese Embassy in Piccadilly, a film enthusiast, Brian had located in a systematic trawl through their computerized records the name of a Dutch lawyer who had worked in the defence team at the Tokyo Trial of Japanese war criminals in 1947, after which he had settled in the port of Yokohama for the rest of his life. This man had met Ozu when the director was shooting an official film of the trial and they had become friends. An instructive body of information emerged from following this lead, the credit for which Brian insisted remain anonymous and the BFI curator, in his introductory address from the stage of a sold-out NFT 1, thanked enthusiastically 'a dedicated private researcher'.

Jack had guessed the researcher was Brian but said nothing until the other regulars had turned for home and the two friends were left walking alone together to Waterloo. Embarrassed by Jack's praise, Brian maintained he had done no more than point the BFI in the right direction.

The rise from one to two films a night was effortlessly achieved, Brian found, made practicable in terms of time because the BFI was free of both advertisements and trailers in its wide choice from at least two sittings every day in each of the three cinemas, plus the Studio, a normal daily menu of eight different movies. The ease with which Brian slid into the new routine reassured him, happening without a specific decision, unusual for him, no plan, exponentially, in a natural response to the circumstances.

140

Brian was often the only regular attending the early film. He had not thought of himself as the oldest buff, but with Jack and the others still at work he accepted that this might indeed be so, after Ephraim's departure.

How old was Jack?

Old enough to have arthritis in his left knee and a slight limp.

Brian felt that he, in fact, looked the younger of the two. He accepted that this might not be how it seemed to others.

Maybe Jack was indeed older and stayed on beyond retirement age in the back room of the travel agency because he needed a weekly wage. Could he still be supporting in some way his estranged daughter?

In the past Brian would have puzzled for hours, days, on a similar unresolved doubt, slept badly and developed a stomach ache. Now, wrapped in his pensioner's cloak, he shrugged and moved along, forgot about the minor query. If he had noticed that he was not worrying, he would have worried about not noticing sooner. Instead, eyes brighter by the month, Brian quietly got on with things. Retirement, he decided, was what he had been working for all along.

Some of the anxiety he used to feel had also receded about when and where to buy things he needed. With ageing circulation, his feet regularly grew so cold at night that he was kept awake and wanted to find two extra-large pairs of soft, thick pure wool socks to wear in bed. The satisfaction of finding with relative ease exactly what he needed was considerable. In acceptable colours too, one pair flecked grey the other flecked brown, from a specialist wool shop on Marylebone Lane.

There were unexpected rewards also in the cinema, he found, films he had never heard of before which left him with warm feelings, thematically supportive of the limitations to his own way of life. Such as *Sugarbaby*, written and directed in Munich in 1985 by Percy Adlon, re-shown at the BFI, a funny, loving and optimistic film, with its encouragement to anyone who felt irremediably handicapped by what had happened to them and by their outward failure to deal with this effectively.

Over the first six months of retirement Brian undertook an ordered examination of the five ring-box files full of BFI programmes, refusing to pass anything to the read-pile until he could honestly recall the look of the film described in the text, turning to varied reference sources if the programme notes failed to summon a convincing image.

One of the many film-things Brian was reminded about while working through his files was how thrilling the finest of those first viewings had been, sometimes expected, by reputation, on other occasions an unheralded masterpiece. There were some very good European directors whose names had not, not then, hit the headlines. Praised by discerning critics on original release, before Brian was a buff, he had seen their films later, coming to them fresh, untutored, as if new. He was reminded during methodical inspection of his five ring-box files of Ermanno Olmi's *The Tree of Wooden Clogs*, well reviewed when made in the late 1970s but suffering a period of neglect at the time Brian had seen it in the Studio, maybe ten people in the audience, several of them fellow buffs. He remembered the film being like nothing he had ever seen before, recalled being left speechless and hurrying from the foyer with an emotional backward wave to the others, silenced by the experience.

Hidden riches.

Maurice Pialat was another undervalued director, his

Loulou recently seen by Brian for the first time, a provocative film, with perfect performances by Isabelle Huppert and Gérard Depardieu.

Before drink and fame wrecked Depardieu's acting – fame then drink, the more likely. And arrogance.

The quality of Pialat's filmmaking which appealed to Brian was its economy, its unhurried humanity, nothing forced, clever but never conceited.

Brian was eager to catch the new Mike Leigh and Ken Loach films, part of the BFI season billed as British Social Realism.

A term he disliked. Posh, pretentious.

Movies about people today, a better description.

Though this Leigh movie, *Mr Turner*, happened to be historical, Timothy Spall already awarded Best Actor at Cannes, after taking oil painting classes at art school in order to play with conviction the great painter.

In the foyer afterwards, Brian and Jack shared their enthusiasm for the score, by the theatre and television composer Gary Yershon, small scale music, no period pomp, modern in its introverted melancholy, much as the artist must have been as a man, Brian suggested. Jack said he recognized the Dutch actress-wife of his Iranian boss in Streatham, near the start of the film chatting in Frisian dialect to a friend and running along the bank of a dyke where Spall was filmed painting en plein-air – shot on the Norfolk Broads not a Texel polder as purported. The new Loach, *Jimmy's Hall*, also had an historical setting, County Leitrim in the 1930s on the border with Northern Ireland, everlasting bigotry and bitterness polluting the narrative. Brian felt bruised by Loach's quiet anger, a film both lyrical and political, the score of new and found material arranged by George Fenton, musical director on a dozen Loach projects, a composition by whom Jack had once heard performed live in concert.

Insensitive to the film, one of the regulars came out in the foyer afterwards with a tasteless delayed suggestion for their South Bank Award: the fake hand from Wayne Wang's *Life is Cheap... But Toilet Paper Is Expensive*.

Brian held his breath, to stifle a rebuke.

The British Social Realism season included the film made by Scottish director Jon S. Baird from the Irvine Welsh novel *Filth*, which Brian attended in order to see Jim Broadbent play a mad psychiatrist, with big blue staring eyes and a wonky bowtie. Such a versatile and endearing actor, leading Jack to come up with a Broadbent story connected to his boss's wife. One of her first professional engagements when she moved to England, at the ICA in the late 1970s, had apparently been in *The Warp*, in which Broadbent had played four different parts, including a Lincolnshire fruit-seller. Lasting twenty-two hours, a saga of hippydom, the play was directed by Ken Campbell, the ferret-down-the-trousers man, a devotee of the accidental.

Bill Nighy was in the play too, Jack said. Nighy and Broadbent the same age, born in 1949 in Caterham and Horton cum Beckering, respectively, Jack added. A year younger than him.

Brian smiled. He and Jack were contemporaries, after all.

Jack said his boss said that Campbell had said one night: 'Wasn't it great, that bit when Mitch fell off the stage and they all adlibbed like crazy till he could climb back on!'

Campbell had given to Jack's boss's wife a copy of his punk poems, printed at the London Poly in an edition of fifty. The title, *Terror, Terror: A Book of Poems are Invitations to Jump in the Lake*, was typical Ken, Jack said.

It's only true if it makes you laugh, Jack's boss had told him that Ken used to say.

Brian frowned, thinking that it was the sort of remark Jack himself was celebrated for making. Until then he had not heard of Ken Campbell and was yet again astounded by how much Jack knew about so many things and people.

Spall and Broadbent were definitely his favourite British actors, Brian announced post-screening of *Filth*. At the moment, he added, aware how easily swayed he was by the latest film seen.

In his pre-BFI existence Brian used to spend every spare moment during Wimbledon fortnight watching tennis on television. The pat-pat of the ball back and forth across the net captured his attention, inescapably, glued him to the set till the late-night recap and analysis. Uninterested in tennis as a game and indifferent to the so-claimed personalities of the sport, Brian nonetheless retained a certain nostalgic affection for the Championship and in the sunny summer of his first full year of retirement decided to treat himself to a day out at the All England Lawn Tennis Club down in Wimbledon.

Direct on the District Line by return to Embankment he was sure to be back at the BFI in time for at least one evening film.

Brian booked in advance a seat on Centre Court for one of the men's semi-finals and bought a floppy sun-hat with neck protection hanging at the back. The least creased of his blue jackets, smartest tie and an ironed white shirt would fit in nicely with the traditional ethos of Wimbledon, as he perceived it to be. Wrongly, it turned out, dress standards not what they were in Brian's TV watching days – over twenty-five years ago, he realized, as he wandered in a daze through the carefree crowds of noisy young people.

Young to him, Brian corrected, abruptly unsure how old most of them actually were, many of the women spectators ageless in loose designer shorts.

On recognizing the obsequious Hugh Grant weaving a path towards the tea tent, a bronzed starlet on either arm, Brian hurried in the opposite direction to reach the safety of his reserved seat. In his judgement, *Bridget Jones's Diary* was one of the worst films he had ever made the mistake of seeing, for which Grant's caricature acting was largely to blame. The tennis itself, however, was more entertaining than he had feared it might be, the women as awesomely athletic as the men, and so determined, so competitive. Brian took his hat off to them – literally not figuratively, his hasty purchase too tight and sweaty. The men's semi-final held on Brian's court was between a Serbian and a Bulgarian, neither of whom were prominent names. On the strength of recently seeing an excellent short film by Bulgarian co-directors Grozeva and Valchanov, a wife and husband team, he rooted for their fellow countryman Grigor Dimitrov. The tennis was dull, and Brian spent part of the time thinking about their film, *Jump*, in which a female water-metre-reader called at a flat temporarily in the care of a confirmed bachelor and there followed what Brian remembered as the most deceitful, most passionate, the funniest and the saddest of love affairs.

Dimitrov lost the match and Brian returned to the South Bank in plenty of time for his movie – Jarmusch's *Only Lovers Left Alive*, on its first London showing after success in Cannes.

Every three or four years since her death Brian had visited his mother's grave in Rochester. The least inadequate of his parents, it was she who had rescued him – and herself – from the suffering of Northern Ireland.

Eventually, not soon enough.

Never mind. He felt grateful for small mercies where she was concerned.

Now he had retired, Brian was able to take a weekday train down to Kent, no longer resenting the loss of precious weekend time, choosing a sunny summer's day and first toiling up to the ramparts of the Castle for its old-English view across the Medway Estuary. At the cemetery someone from her church, Brian presumed, had filled the empty metal vase with a large bunch of purple plastic roses. He lent his skinny bottom to rest against the arched top of her porphyry gravestone, trying to think kindly of his mother and the stream of fugitive Ulster Volunteer Force paramilitaries she used to hide and feed before delivering at night to a clandestine boat in Ramsgate harbour.

Hard though it was to be her son, Brian admired in retrospect her strength of purpose, her commitment to the community in which she believed, however brutal their methods.

That's how Belfast was.

Look at his father.

Publicly denounced his dissident wife as she was led away pregnant to prison, where Brian was born and from where, aged less than a year, he was removed to an orphanage. She had only let herself become pregnant this second time by the miserable man, his mother had once told him, in the hope of avoiding arrest. To no avail.

Neither his dad nor elder bother Peter had ever visited Brian in the orphanage.

In the cemetery he had difficulty reading the inscription carved in Gothic lettering on the expensive stone, an Old Testament text which he had never fully understood, erected by people he did not know. Alone beside the grave Brian began to giggle. Softly at first, then quite loudly, caught by a picture of the scene near the end of *The Cook,*

147

the Thief, His Wife & Her Lover, of the roasted body of the lover borne in funereal procession to the dinner table by six white-clad chefs, accompanied by the escalating tension of Michael Nyman's 'Memorial' with its saxophone surge and the purest extended notes of a high soprano.

He was tempted to travel a couple more stops on the train along the coast to Birchington-on-Sea and visit Ephraim for an impromptu tea, the anticipated pleasure of seeing the old regular again defeated by Brian's fear of the unexpected, and he went straight back to town as usual.

After stopping work Brian had continued to call at Il Castelletto for lunch and a chat, quite often, usually on a Tuesday when Lorenzo's Mum's lasagne was at its freshly baked best. He also kept to his six-weekly appointment nearby with Joe, the Cypriot barber, their conversation following a well-worn track, reassuringly familiar, Joe reporting on seasonal progress in his allotment and Brian describing an appealing film he had recently seen. He enjoyed hearing from Joe about the annual repetition of planting, growing and harvesting, reassured by the existence of another's ritual. They agreed on many things in general, arbitrary bank fees a regular gripe. When charges on ATM cash withdrawals came in Brian had stopped using wall machines altogether and always went inside to a cashier to remove money straight from his account, seldom more than twenty pounds at a time.

Safer, anyway, regardless of fees, he said.

Doesn't matter, but they dropped ATM charges some time ago, Joe pointed out.

On the bus home it occurred to Brian that barbers chose mostly to agree with what their customers said, whether they actually did or not – good for business, and for the heart, cutting out arguments and their assault on ageing blood-pressure.

Retirement made no difference to the clothes Brian wore, kitted out each day as if off to the office. Important to maintain standards, block the danger of a slide down the slippery slope to food stains and elbow patches, he used to tell himself. Confident at long last of his rightful place amongst the buffs, Brian was ready to admit that, in truth, he considered none of them properly dressed, drab at best, semi-derelict at worst, not a primary colour in sight on top and a forest of fawn trousers below, either too long or too short. Ephraim had been the exception, always smartly turned out. He used to wear a pressed three-piece charcoal grey suit and embroidered kippah, and, Brian suspected, a tallit beneath his waistcoat, black and white wool tassels occasionally exposed. Being Jewish made no noticeable difference as to which films Ephraim had been prepared to watch, science fiction his specialist field – although his all-time favourite movie was *The Full Monty*, in which he self-parodyingly claimed to have spotted that two of the unemployed Sheffield steel workers were circumcised. Another of the regulars rode a drop-handled bicycle and wore shorts the year round. Brian regarded this as both absurd and somewhat unattractive, frowning at the parade of hairy thighs and T-shirt perspiration. These irritating habits he forgave, however, out of respect for the bicyclist's expertise on modern Oriental war movies – European war movies set in the Orient to be precise. They often compared post-screen notes and opinions, dovetailing their related areas of expertise.

Thinking of *The Full Monty*, Brian recalled that for ages after seeing the film Robert Carlyle had been his favourite actor, undisguised in public about his rage against the power of wealth, the greed always for more. Brian took a memory-note to catch up with Carlyle's latest films. Not to forget John Hurt either: the alien bursting from his stomach! What was he doing these days?

Brian became aware one evening that Jack was cutting his hair shorter, both at the front and behind his ears, and wondered how long this had been going on without his noticing. His friend's untidy head of hair had grown thinner and greyer with the passing years, his beard streaked white. In contrast Brian's own obsession with a clean shave had intensified with age and he now carried everywhere in his leather bag, as well as a travelling toothbrush and small tube of toothpaste, a battery-operated minirazor, at sheltered moments turning aside to give his cheeks and chin a quick going-over, rendering his bland face eternally pale and pristine.

One of the benefits of being a buff, from Brian's perspective, was that whatever their backgrounds, age or profession they spoke to each other in the same language, centred on cinema. Knowing that in conversation they shared tone and approach as well as a common vocabulary minimized misunderstanding. By and large the words they used meant the same to each of them, which might explain why he had not noticed that the man with a flat behind Westminster Cathedral was different and had thus made the error of accepting an invitation to visit him.

The strange bloke still attended BFI films from time to time, but Brian never addressed him directly.

Nor did he Brian.

Which was fine, a kind-of understanding.

A truce, at least.

Jack, more observant than Brian of the people around him, described the man as a time bomb waiting to go off.

Amongst the buffs it was Jack who made the most imaginative use of words, holding robust views on language. Critics' jargon was his main bugbear, convinced that their complicated prose was difficult to follow mostly because they did not understand the films they were writing about. Out to impress by their brilliance, it was the least interesting clever-clever films which received their dubious praise. Jack objected stridently also to outsider misuse of the words 'obsession' or 'fetish' to label people like him who liked, a lot, watching a particular kind of film. And not-watching, too, he added, conscious of his friend Brian's dislike of on-camera danger to eyes, Buñuel-style. Only the other day they had seen Toshio Matsumoto's *Funeral Parade of Roses*, in which near the end the transvestite protagonist stabbed out both of his own eyes with a kitchen knife, to blind himself from witnessing his lover's infidelity. Although Brian had lowered his gaze from this well-signposted scene, he was nevertheless impressed by the film's freedom of expression for its time, impossible in contemporary 1960s Britain for gay sex scenes such as these to be publicly shown, naked and uninhibited.

Daring enough forty years later, to Brian's taste.

Luis Buñuel split the buffs in three: some uninterested, some devoted, and others able take him or leave him. Brian was in the latter camp, in this instance. When the director's *That Obscure Object of Desire* appeared in the monthly brochure, he decided it was time for him to see this classic, partly swayed by Jack's mellow enthusiasm. He was really pleased to have gone, able for the first time to watch Buñuel and not mind feeling bewildered, understanding that it was not the filmmaker's intention to make a fool of him and suspecting that Buñuel himself knew not much more than he did about how things were meant to turn out. Instead of being annoyed by the conceit of casting simultaneously two actresses of the same age in the single part of Conchita, Brian found it fun, a seventy-seven-year-old veteran filmmaker making merited merriment.

Delighted that Brian liked the film, in the foyer afterwards Jack confirmed that Buñuel had indeed left quite a bit to chance on the set, as illustrated in the scene where the character Mathieu – played by Fernando Rey – grabbed a heavy jute sack, lifted it onto his back and walked off down the lane out of shot. Apparently Buñuel only thought of this at the last moment, an action of no narrative relevance, and for safety's sake he had then filmed a second take without the sack. The actors and director had all agreed on viewing the day's rushes that the first instinctual version had worked much the best.

Jack repeated Buñuel's comment that he could not explain why one way of shooting a scene turned out better than another, that in fact he did not want to know and to risk the loss of the magic of making films.

As he had been years ago with Eastwood's *The Outlaw Josey Wales*, Brian was still from time to time consumed with the desire to see a particular film, his focus of the moment *Holy Motors*, a French movie starring Denis Lavant in eleven different roles, recently described by *Sight & Sound* as a 'loose-limbed acrobatic genius'. There was no sign yet of it being screened at the BFI and Brian was briefly tempted to break ranks and catch the newly released film at the ICA down on The Mall, where it was showing at the weekend.

In the end he remained loyal to the South Bank.

Sooner or later, *Holy Motors* was bound to turn up on home ground.

The next Saturday afternoon in a bookshop on Charing Cross Road, Brian thought he spotted Jack inspecting the narrow stacks at the far end of the basement. In their usual surroundings at the BFI, he would have identified him instantly, but in the world outside things looked different.

Was it him, or a tall thin stranger, magenta socks showing beneath his trousers?

Brian tiptoed down the aisle of books to get a closer look, freezing as the man looked up and smiled.

It *was* Jack, what a relief!

After making their separate purchases they walked down the road towards Trafalgar Square to take tea and apple cake at Gaby's, quizzing each other as to how often they each went to Any Amount of Books and, since in both cases the answer was quite often, wondering how they had not bumped into each other there previously. Once seated at a table in the small deli they showed each other what they had bought, Brian laying out on the scrubbed Formica the five postcards of old picture houses he had extracted from amongst the ephemera in a drawer beneath the stairs in the bookshop, including one of the Olympia Cinema on the prom at Southend-on-Sea, with crowded boating lake in the foreground. Given his musical interests, Jack could barely believe his luck in finding, tucked inside a late 1970s edition of *Empty Words* by John Cage, which he was intending to buy anyway, the invitation to a performance of the composer's *Music for 15 Harps* in the garden at MoMA in New York in 1985, together with a cutting from the *New York Times*:

> It is hard to imagine a better fitting of event to environment than Friday evening's 'Garden of Harps' in the Sculpture Garden of the Museum of Modern Art. Fifteen harpists, all in white, played music which filled up the night air pleasantly, without trying too terribly hard to carve out its own definite space.

This flimsy bit of paper took forty years to make its way from Manhattan to the Charing Cross Road and is now en route to Tooting, Jack said. Miraculous!

Found a few yards from where the London Film-makers' Co-op or Co-operative gave its first screenings in the 1960s, in the basement of nearby Better Books, Brian volunteered.

Serendipity. Aren't connections a delight? Jack responded, shaking his thinning head of long grey hair. Everything is connected, if you look hard enough.

After sharing their pleasure in bargain purchases, they also talked tangentially around the subject of maybe meeting up again for a concert, better still, Jack seemed to imply, a return tea at Brian's flat, already almost fifteen years since they had exchanged names and met up in Tooting, ten years before that when they had first registered each other's presence as regulars at the BFI, during which extended time a special friendship had slowly grown.

No, Brian unhesitatingly said. Sorry, it's just not possible. Let's stick to the BFI, please.

On Saturday evenings Jack sometimes also booked in for two films and, although they were too early for their different first shows, they quickly finished their tea, negotiated the traffic in the Strand, walked down the cobbled lane beside Charing Cross Main Line Station, through Embankment ticket hall and up onto the footbridge across the river to the South Bank.

Richard Rogers, you know, Jack said.

He designed the bridge?

No, I had no idea, Brian admitted.

Brian stuck his head firmly into a book while they sat waiting for their films to commence. When the tannoy finally called him to the cinema Brian was pleased to find his ticket stub collected by his favourite usherette, the colour of whose hair had changed since he had last seen her from pink to yellow. He mentioned this, proposing that the new lemon yellow suited her, with its hint of green. Looking directly into the black-clad young woman's sparkling eyes, seemingly amused by the old regular's spry comment, Brian briefly wondered what the people at the BFI thought of him and the other buffs. Before dismissing such reflections as pointless.

The film turned out to be a rarity, a Japanese movie that Brian disliked.

Seijun Suzuki's *Gate of Flesh* was set in Tokyo in the years immediately after the war, when the country was occupied by Allied troops, with the Emperor under house arrest. Unwilling to write off any Japanese film, Brian spent the spare twenty minutes before his next screening in a comfortable chair near the box office, eyes closed, mentally removing what he saw as imperfections, marginally altering a few other bits, and then rerunning at speed the new version in his head. In this case the main problem, from Brian's outlook, was the colour, shot 'magnificently' – the programme note said – in Scope but which he wanted to be black and white, the classic medium of the period.

Too deeply respectful of directors to imagine making a film himself, he could, he felt, in a different life perhaps have been an assistant editor.

After a quick sweep of the razor across his chin Brian walked briskly, head angled forward, to NFT 2 for *Being John Malkovich*, which he was not expecting to enjoy. And tried not to, unable in the end to resist the cinematic appeal of Lotte's longing for Maxine.

On the way home in the tube he realized that the awkwardness over tea with Jack had put him in a negative frame of mind, and that maybe he needed to sample *Gate of Flesh* a second time, before writing up its report in his file index.

Brian was aware that this degree of self-understanding was unusual for him. He secretly hoped that a regime of balanced good sense might be emerging with retirement.

One of the other buffs, youngish with tiny delicate hands, kept a running list of the films he had seen with great endings, nine to date in his personal judgement, noted in the order of his original viewing. Like Brian, convinced of the impossibility of comparing on merit crime film with comedy, say, the fellow buff resented the mania for ranking best this and that of the year, films or footballers. Though, for Brian, if endings had to be listed in order of preference, *The Far Road* would be near the top, at the conclusion of which the disgruntled Japanese railway worker stood on the shoreline beside his wife and held in his hand his long-service presentation watch, a cheap insult, he felt, and asked rhetorically: 'How far can I throw it?'

As this emblem of labour exploitation plopped into the sea they laughed companionably, after their thirty harsh and hard-working years of marriage charted in the film. The credits appeared as their heads bent towards each other, a few frames after the splash of the watch.

The young buff's interests leant – understandably – towards more contemporary movies and one of his favourite endings, he told Brian, was to Claire Denis' *Beau Travail*, in which a French legionnaire, physically strong and self-assured, danced alone in a night club in Djibouti, his vulnerability gradually becoming apparent, revealed in the final shots to be close to internal disintegration.

It was this same actor whom Brian was longing to see in *Holy Motors*.

156

First films were always better than the director's last, the buff claimed.

Always? Brian queried.

Yes, absolutely always.

The certainty of youth, Brian murmured to himself. So decisive.

The death of Silien – played by a young Jean-Paul Belmondo – in *The Finger Man* was a pretty good way to end a movie too, in the garden room of the jewel thief's own house in Seine-et-Marne, silent, littered with corpses.

Dead-end. Nothing more to say.

In Brian's private film pantheon, the one ending to rival *The Far Road* was the conclusion of *Tokyo Story*, when Kyoko complained fiercely about the selfishness of her family, an emotional outburst to which her sister-in law Noriko responded with a shrug, proclaiming that hurt was inevitable.

Isn't life disappointing? Kyoko then said.

Yes, Noriko replied, smiling.

By the time of this, the final exchange of the film the audience already knew that Kyoko's young brother, the husband of beautiful Noriko, was missing presumed dead, the ship on which he had been serving sunk without trace two years earlier by the Americans during the final days of the war.

Notes and lists were an essential armoury for most of the regulars.

Taking up a subject recommended by the young buff, one of their colleagues did indeed list best first films, noting down his selection of champion directorial debuts. For which it was widely agreed there was little to rival Bresson's *Angels of Sin*, made in Paris when still under Nazi occupation, set in a secluded convent in which the nuns illegally harboured women from the street, a moving film, both erotic and spiritual. Many of the most memorable films like *Angels of Sin* tended to be several things at the same time, with no need to take sides one way or the other.

The war years were an incredible time for French cinema, in Brian's view, Henri-Georges Clouzot's *Le Corbeau* another amongst several major movies.

And Marcel Carné with *Les Enfants du Paradis*, Jack's favourite. Everlastingly beautiful, he once said.

The second time Brian had seen this film he shed a tear to match the Pierrot's.

One of the other regulars had decided to list the best meals eaten on camera. Their listings were never simple, all sorts of detailed information added in, such as the star actors in a director's first movie, the time of day or night of the great beginnings and endings, the length of screen-time of the crucial meal and brief sketches of the fictional characters in the selected scenes.

Tarantino's *Jackie Brown* currently reigned as Brian's top beginning, behind the roll of the opening credits the wonderful long walk of the air hostess in her sky blue suit down the mosaic wall of the airport, seen from the waist up, breaking into a run to reach the departure gate in time. Brian had barely heard of Pam Grier before Tarantino worked his film magic and for a while he day-dreamed of nobody else, so intensely alive on screen.

Some of the regulars were fact-addicts in their list-making, preoccupied with film minutiae, the mechanics and figures of production, whereas Brian and the buff with small hands cared principally about the aesthetic intentions of director and actors and the resultant look of a film. Information was important to Brian for the sake of historical understanding but not for any intrinsic value in facts as facts.

This was another of the wonderful things about film, Brian reminded himself, the limitless legitimate points of approach, all interesting, all worth discussion.

The benevolence of buffery, in a curious phrase of Jack's.

The number of buffs attending the BFI began for a variety of reasons to fall off, until within three years of his retirement only half a dozen intermittent regulars remained, seldom all present, Brian the only one turning up without fail every night, in his case usually for two films.

DVDs were to blame, he reckoned, with Blockbuster Video renting out material at low cost, poor prints insensitively cut and edited. Netflix Subscription was the new offender in the marketplace, streaming classic movies on home computer screens and TVs.

The postcard of a painting. Cheapskate copy of the real thing, Brian recalled Jack grumbling about small screen viewing.

The mobile phone was also to blame, Brian believed, though with little direct experience himself. The first buff to carry a mobile had worked for BT, a switchboard operator who was given the then-coveted gadget as a loyalty present by the company. Brian was relieved at the time not to feel the need for a mobile of his own, as he seldom either made or received a telephone call. With the addition of other services – street maps, weather forecast, text messages and the rest – he considered changing his mind and visited an Apple store. Confused by the myriad choice of type and style of device, and startled by the prices, he decided he did not want one after all. Recently, in a flurry of indecision, he had looked again at the mobile phone market, taken by the idea of storing photos of his entire collection of cinema postcards, to have at hand to refer to when out and about and thus avoid the error of duplicate purchases. On his third visit to a discount warehouse in Tottenham Court Road, Brian bought the simplest model available, formal in his gratitude to the patient young assistant, his boyhood stutter briefly returning, as still happened from time to time in a public context.

In an unexpected turn of events, on arriving early at the BFI on several cold winter afternoons Brian came across a homeless women seated on the carpeted floor in a dead-end corner beyond the fire exit, barricaded within a circle of possessions stuffed into plastic bags, more than it looked possible to carry in two hands.

Maybe she tied the handles together with the blue twine currently wrapped in several turns around her waist and slung the bags across her shoulders, Brian speculated.

Like an urban milkmaid.

Or had she secreted somewhere out there in the street nearby a battered supermarket trolley, to reacquisition when the time came to be ejected from her temporary refuge, as she inevitably would be, sooner rather than later.

Brian stopped and stared, ready to depart the moment she noticed him. Unperturbed, a Michelin figure in multiple layers of clothing and two woollen earflap hats one on top of the other on her head, the woman pursued her endless sorting and shifting of the bags, two of which, Brian noticed, were full to the brim of empty plastic bags.

In case she ran short?

He stepped quietly back into the main lobby and left her in peace.

Then, one January night two weeks later, on his way post-film to Waterloo and home to sleep, he spotted the woman in a rain-protected corner beneath the bottom flight of concrete steps up to the bridge over to Somerset House. She appeared to be fast asleep, seated with heavy cloth-wrapped legs outstretched, arms embracing her circle of bags and leaning against a metal trolley with missing wheel.

He and the other buffs were her, Brian plainly saw, were it not for the sanctuary of film.

In describing this incident to Jack and admitting his own perennial nightmare of destitution, Brian almost also told him of his mother's furious repeated warning that unless – in her exact words – he 'pulled his socks up' he would eventually be homeless, out on the streets.

An unexpected reminder of Brian's faraway past arrived in the post one morning, the invitation to his secondary school in Rochester's centenary celebrations. He felt flattered to be asked, having flown the place when just sixteen to begin his apprenticeship at a small firm of accountants in Clerkenwell, Irish friends of his mother's. She had died two months later and he had abandoned accountancy, setting him off on a forever solitary journey, the hostel in St Pancras first of his many addresses. Brian filled in affirmatively the school's reply card and posted it on the way to his weekly shop for food at the Sainsbury's by the canal in Camden, a building with the futuristic industrial glamour of a film set, he had always felt, admired since watching from work it take shape twenty-five years earlier. The moment Brian had dropped into the post box the letter to his old school he knew he had made a mistake.

Not important, he said to himself. Let it rest.

Which he did, threw their follow-up letters unopened into the wastepaper basket beneath the desk in his small sitting room, until they eventually stopped coming. He did wonder how on earth, and from whom, they had obtained his address.

Familial contact severed, a number of phrases nevertheless survived from his boyhood, remembered by

Brian and repeated to himself at apposite moments over the years. 'OUR TRUE INTENT IS ALL FOR YOUR DELIGHT' was one of them, seen when he was eleven, taken by his mother to what was supposed to be a special treat – ten days at Butlins Holiday Camp in Skegness – these words embossed in big bright letters above the entrance to the poolside café. Brian had hated every minute there. Hated his mother for forcing him to join multiple activities for boys. Hated the Red Coats and their mean-mouthed abuse when adult backs were turned. Hated himself for not being able to swim.

Apart from sporadic minor interventions, Brian's London life had continued in its daily pattern unevent-fully through the three years and five months since retirement, until the night came at the BFI when he was no longer able to conceal, from himself or from Jack, dif-ficulties with his sight. It had begun with watering in his left eye towards the end of a two-hour film, discomfort which cleared within minutes of beginning the foyer get-together. Putting the problem down to a temporary infection, Brian had mentioned it to no-one, assuming the eye would right itself in a few days. It did not. The weeping worsened, occurred earlier and earlier in the screenings, until the waterfall in his left eye distorted his whole vision. He tried holding a hand over the bad eye and looking at the film solely through the other but, on its own, the right eye blurred the moving image. There came a point when he spent more time trying to see than he did actually looking, which prevented him from meaningful contribution to their after-film discussions. Though the buffs seldom made direct personal comments, Jack sur-prised Brian one night by asking, in front of the others, if he was alright, given his relative silence. Shocked into an instant response, Brian blurted out the truth and was astonished by the real concern of several buffs, as well as by Jack's confession that his large bifocal spectacles were a result of the similar problem he had suffered a few years back. He recommended the optician in Tooting who had sorted him out, and noted down for Brian the telephone number and address on the back of one of the travel brochures in his carrier bag.

Contrary to his habitual claim of reasonable eyesight, tests revealed to Brian his inability to see almost anything clearly, the optician's slick swopping of lenses transforming his vision of the letters on her wall chart. The passage of dots across the video screen had initially been almost invisible and the optician – a breezy young woman – had the temerity to suggest that scrupulous use of her prescribed glasses might improve his posture too. He obediently ordered the three divergent pairs she recommended, one for everyday normal, another for reading, and a third for live watching of movies. Brian chose the cheapest contrasting frames available and cases of differing design to make it easier for him to identify which was which.

In the foyer before the film on the evening after they had arrived at the flat by courier, Jack patted him on the arm on spotting the new spectacles. Brian did not see the gesture coming, and flinched, until realizing it was Jack, in sympathy not threat.

One of the other buffs, as thin and tall as Jack, with a brick red birthmark across the side of his face, asked if it had occurred to any of the others that the temperature at the BFI had sunk a little low. Although two of the regulars expressed sympathy for their colleague finding the cinema chilly, they and all the others, Brian included, stated their preference for an auditorium too cold rather than too hot, to lessen the danger after a tiring day's work

163

of nodding off. Jack suggested that his fellow buff pack a lightweight rug in his knapsack to wrap around his legs during the films.

Now that Jack had mentioned the idea, Brian wondered about doing the same himself, his feet turning icy cold by the end of every day, whatever the weather.

The film playing that night was *Strictly Ballroom*, by an Australian, not exactly Brian's kind of thing but in the relief of being able to see properly he adored it, enthusing to the others afterwards that it had a touch of Alan Parker's *Fame* with an echo of Merchant Ivory's *Roseland*, plus entirely its own noisy exuberance. Two of the buffs said, in semi-unison, that it was good to have him back on form.

Jack did a nice witty thing, proposing to Brian that they book in together to a screening the following week of *Koyaanisquatsi*. Even if Brian was unable to see the film too well, at least he would have the Philip Glass music to enjoy listening to, Jack quipped.

With the NFT 1 screen at its widest and the images so colourful and vigorous, on the *Koyaanisquatsi* night Brian was as overwhelmed as Jack by the total experience, with Glass's relentlessly overlapping score masterful in its own right, whilst perfectly attuned to the non-narrative film. Incredible shots of the Grand Canyon and Monument Valley fused with sections in Chicago of a full moon sailing behind skyscrapers. Eighty-six minutes of paradise.

Opera as film, Jack described it.

During these first post-optician days Brian tried his best to moderate the overwhelming relief he felt at the effect of his spectacles and at the pleasure of recovering his sense of togetherness with the reduced band of buffs. Unable to see cinema clearly, his self-esteem had plummeted and he had condemned himself as unworthy of them all. Miraculously, equanimity was restored. He could stop pretending, relax again to watching film and to chatting confidently with his friends.

He sailed through unscathed the potential dual-upset of both Ireland and ageing in Rampling's latest film *45 Years*, coloured by the County Antrim boyhood of the writer and director Andrew Haigh's long-term partner. On another night, after picking himself up from the disappointment of discovering that *Manchester by the Sea* was set in Massachusetts rather than Lancashire, Brian admired this new film too, riding out the painful descriptions of community alienation.

In buoyant spirits Brian later in the week entered Il Castelletto for his occasional lunch with a resounding salute to all and sundry.

Blimey, Brian! Won the pools? Lorenzo called out.

Tony was in, with his youngest son, who the other day had become a fully qualified anaesthetist, and Brian sat down on a spare chair at their table. They were celebrating with a bottle of wine from the Co-op and a dish of pan-fried calamari with garlic and lemon rustled up by Dario. The father told Brian how his son used to stop off at Il Castelletto after school and wait in the corner with a coke, doing his homework, until Tony had finished the day's local plumbing job and called to collect the boy. Sometimes, if work went well, it was the other way round and Tony waited for his son to finish school, swopping indie music news with Lorenzo. Brian declined to acknowledge another of the café's regulars, a man he disliked, who sat at his customary table near the hatch, with his wife, whom he steadily ignored, declining as usual to speak a word to her, the woman's courageous face crumbling in public humiliation at the relentless insult.

As he waited at the counter to pay, Brian noticed a fragile old man standing just inside the door to the street, blinking continuously and wringing his hands. He wore a fairly clean white shirt, without pullover or jacket, and on his feet a scuffed pair of hiking boots. Turning from the table he was serving Lorenzo also noticed the man and greeted him by name, straight away walking over to speak to him, holding the cold hands in both of his to calm their nervous movement. Brian could not hear what they said to each other, though at one point the man tried to leave and Lorenzo would not allow him to, insisting he wait while he fetched his dark blue donkey jacket from its hanger behind the counter and gave it to the man, placing his arms in the sleeves and doing up the buttons. A smile finally lightened the old man's face and he agreed to sit down at a spare table near the door, where Lorenzo brought him a mug of tea.

What's an old coat to me? he said, ringing the till for Brian's bill.

To celebrate being able to see again, and at the same time give his three new spectacles a test outing, Brian made a day trip to Petworth House, something he had wanted to do for years and had always put off as never the right weekend for what had felt to him at the time like quite an undertaking. Logistical problems remained, not least getting there, the National Trust's directions assuming arrival by car, abandoning people like Brian to research the details of a seventy-five-minute train journey from Victoria to Pulborough and local bus on to Petworth.

Worth it, though, for Turner.

Almost anything was, Brian told himself, his cheerful mood holding.

Brian already knew, from books and postcards, some of the paintings of the palatial house and deer park commissioned from Turner by the Earl of Egremont. Drawn

166

primarily to the work of filmic grandeur, Brian was longing to see in the flesh *The Lake, Petworth, Sunset: Fighting Bucks*, a bucolic scene dramatized beneath a thick yellow, red and gold sky covering over half of the five feet wide canvas. He had made a special effort to visit on this occasion because, for the first time since the Earl's lifetime, most of Turner's Petworth paintings had been gathered from dispersal around the world for exhibition in the house.

He felt spoilt by the riches of the show. Particularly, contrary to expectation, by Turner's diminutive watercolours of the grand interiors, including the large library in which the painter set up studio on each of his visits. His last work at Petworth, a watercolour, was of Lord Egremont lying in his coffin in the salon, awaiting internment in the family mausoleum.

When everything went to plan, as on his day out to Petworth, Brian felt actively proud of himself. Wishing to take a step back and observe with sympathy the strictures of his desire for control, he turned to a movie analogy, relating his behaviour to those method actors who learned their lines assiduously and practised in advance each move and gesture. Not for him or them off-the-cuff invention, nothing as chancy as improvisation. Like some of his favourite movie stars – Robert de Niro, Cate Blanchett, Maggie Smith – Brian rehearsed his moves for the day. In his cinema experience, only the Japanese commonly got away with acting-on-the-spot to camera, supremely in the wild energy of face and body of Tatsuya Nakadai, fifty-two of the one hundred and thirty-six movies in which he appeared Brian had seen, including the first, *The Thick-Walled Room* of 1956 and last, so far, *Lear on the Shore* in 2017. The ambition to tick off on his list of seen cinema a ton of Nakadai's films made survival a necessity.

Latterly Brian's endemic anxiety had focused on repeatedly checking that all three spectacle cases, with the glasses inside, were safe in his bag or jacket pocket, if not there then on his nose, frightened he might have dropped a case in the dark of the auditorium, or left one on a café table. These were not idle fears, for in wielding three sets of spectacles one or other was often temporarily mislaid in the course of a busy two-film evening at the cinema. Brian intended to print his name and address on all three spectacles and also on each case but had not yet done so. He was adept at putting off actions that he could not exactly pre-configure, undecided technically how best to mark the frames to lasting effect.

It was a relief, in a way, to admit that control was an illusion. An innocent abroad, an adult child, Brian was continuously taken by surprise. Measured and careful in his progress through the day, seeking to move at the same pace whatever he did, wherever he went, he watched in awe the girl at the new BFI café counter act with such speed, extracting a tea bag, filling the cup with hot water, pouring milk from the fridge into a mini-jug, placing spoon and sugar sachet in the saucer, and operating the till all in a whirl of blurred movement, as if she had three arms, ready before he was and he had nothing to do except hand over his credit card. She spoke fast too, and clearly, in an Ulster accent. Brian was no longer able to tell from where in the Six Counties she came.

Skilled at cutting off in public and concentrating on the newspaper, Brian tried not to notice things going on around him as he occupied himself till it was time to join the buffs standing in the foyer pre-film. With its decline in size and quality since being issued free under the lazy editorship of a retired Tory Chancellor, the *Evening*

Standard these days often failed to fill the gap, leaving Brian to listen in open-mouthed astonishment to nearby conversations. The other evening it was two well-dressed women, slashed skirts revealing slim silken legs, talking about their children's pets and the bother, to say nothing of the expense, of placing hamsters and kittens and things in care during the family's lengthy summer holidays, one on the Greek islands, the other visiting her husband's parents in Florida. Much the best, they eagerly agreed, to have the animals secretly put down and at the end of the holidays pretend they had died of some bug decimating the cattery.

Brian felt such an idiot in his ignorance about what he presumed must be the relatively ordinary family lives of these two women. After seeing hundreds of films, thousands, in fact, some of them quite daring, the business of parenthood remained a mystery to him.

Who was from outer space, he or them?

Whether due to suppressed worry about his sight, or the revival of some other ancient hurt, Brian had begun intermittently to lose his temper in public, without restraint. In fury one night at a latecomer asking him in a whisper in the dark four minutes into the movie to shift his legs and bag, Brian had hit him with his fist as hard as he could in the stomach. Stifling laughter, the man had stepped lightly right over Brian's locked knees to sit down in a vacant seat further along the row.

Another outburst had erupted in a café on his summer vacation in Southport, where Brian had been joined at the table by a polite young man in a tartan lumber jacket, who before sitting down had enquired if the chair was vacant. On holiday Brian felt at liberty to talk to strangers, something he avoided at home in London, envisioning a host of unpleasant consequences. The topic of cinema soon

169

emerged, and Brian was impressed by the youngster's knowledge, speaking with fervour and precision about some esoteric material and claiming to have seen almost every film Brian mentioned. Southport born, the stranger worked over the river in Manchester, in advertising, and Brian pictured an inner-city artistic quarter with a small Cinematheque where keen young men and women fed their infatuation with cinema. He was incensed to discover that the fake buff had watched all the material he spoke of downloaded to his Apple Mac. Spluttering with rage, Brian told him, in a louder voice than intended, that he had not in fact seen a single one of these films.

The postcard of a picture not the painting, Brian said, paraphrasing Jack.

An aesthetic travesty, he added, before the man had time to reply.

In effect, you're a cheat, Brian shouted, by then addressing the whole hushed café.

He grabbed the handles of his bag and walked out – without paying, he realized as he stood by the breakwater at the end of the road, staring in fury at the chilly sea. Once he felt sure the young man would have left, Brian returned to the café to settle his bill.

Wedded to habit, since retiring Brian had taken all four summer holidays in Southport, during the same July fortnight, an annual swap from cinema to promenade, the retirement reverse of his work-time vacation taken every year at the BFI's London Film Festival. He had originally chosen Southport on the grounds that there used to be seven cinemas in the once-fashionable, now-inexpensive Merseyside resort, of three of which he had old postcards in his collection. Brian knew it was the right decision to make Southport his summer destination when on his first holiday there he had come across a traditional bookshop with bow-fronted windows painted racing green and narrow avenues of packed shelves, on one of which were dozens of boxes of postcards. Flicking slowly through the cache he had picked out three of the four defunct Southport cinemas then missing from his collection and another ten beauties from seaside towns around the coast. Prize of the bunch was the Picturedrome on Lord Street, then the main boulevard, the first purpose-built cinema in town, photographed for this postcard soon after it opened in 1910. It was long gone by the 2010s when Brian had unearthed this antique card after patient thumbing of the oblong cardboard boxes. Normally the early cards which Brian sought were hand-coloured in the lithographic plate, years before colour photography. This black and white postcard of the Picturedrome he found equally enticing, known to the trade as an 'early real-photo' postcard, photographically printed in crisp detail and deep contrast, the disc on the dome in this near-mint example reading as clear as the day it was made: 'The World in Motion. Performances 3. 7. 9. Sundays 8.45.' Seating for seven hundred on a raked floor, a previous owner had written in neat letters in pencil on the back and, in another hand, the fact that the architect was a local man named Fred Campbell.

Four pounds fifty pence.

Not nothing.

Not a lot either, for a gem.

With the discipline necessary for meaningful collecting within such a large subject, Brian confined his purchases to pre-1920 postcards of British cinema façades and interiors. The thought of being defined as a deltiologist bothered him, sounding pretentious, self-important. Categories and titles worried him, a form, he felt, of social control. By now he owned hundreds of early images of cinemas and was contacted on email by ephemera dealers as far away as San Francisco about UK cinema material they came across, aware of his interest. Even so, Brian denied being a collector. He was someone interested in film and also in cinemas, that was all.

Not quite all.

By character an obsessive, Brian conceded.

Keep watch. Stick to routine. Protect against surprise.

On returning to London from holiday, despite the three pairs of glasses carried constantly with him in his zipped bag and worn with religious zeal on the correct occasions, Brian's middle-distance eyesight again began to deteriorate, rapidly, to a state where he could no longer clearly see the films which he sat through at the BFI.

Terrified of what he might be told, rather than return to the optician in Tooting Brian resolved to define alone a way forward, telling nobody about his difficulties. Able with the aid of his reading spectacles to study books and to see things close up on the computer screen, he subscribed to various film streaming services in order to watch where possible the day's films at home before pretending to see them at the BFI. On the night itself he read the programme notes several times before the start of each film and while it was running rehearsed in the dark the comments he considered making afterwards.

After establishing relatively quickly a new regime, Brian recognized value in the fact that he could hear with added clarity the voices and soundtrack, enabling him to extend his already impressive knowledge of film scores. Daring to think of a future, he hoped in time to become something of a connoisseur on the subject.

If nothing else, these changes to the pattern of his days resolved the retirement quandary of how best to fill the mornings, now occupied preparing for his two evening films.

Brian brazened it out, mentioning nothing to Jack and participating in group conversations as before. His comments may have been a little less relevant than previously but the buffs appeared to listen. Jack, who had evidently noticed the change, had looked him in the eye several times, kindly, quizzically, and on each occasion Brian had turned aside.

Brian's fragile confidence began to return and with it a renewed pleasure in film, different from before, a new order of experience. In watching the BFI's more esoteric foreign films Brian found that with the expectation of difficulty he concentrated harder and almost seemed to understand such work better than before.

Becoming primarily a listener made infuriating certain spoken on-screen sounds, issues which had merely irritated Brian in the past. Rounded actorly vowels, for example. Women as well as men, showing off their drama school credentials, with an unpleasant hint of snobbery. Whilst Brian had never been hot on accents, these days he picked out multiple inconsistencies in the course of a single film – not that he minded in the least if the emotions conveyed felt genuine.

At a BFI Q&A some time ago an actor – Brian could not at that moment recall whom, or after which film – had modestly said of his own effective accent in a previewed movie that there were many different Geordie voices and he had now added one more.

Touching and funny. Worth noting.

Wonderful performance, he seemed to remember, the actor's name and face still escaping him.

To mark the death of Abbas Kiarostami, the key director who had stayed behind to work in Tehran after the Islamic Revolution, the BFI mounted a month of movies under the headline '21st Century Iranian Cinema'. The two films which Brian enjoyed the most were both set in taxis, one titled *Taxi* and the other *Ten*, the latter consisting of ten improvised scenes in the day's work of a woman taxi driver, filmed by Kiarostami. Watched on a day when his eyesight was better than usual, Brian took special pleasure in Jafar Panahi's *Taxi*, made illegally after the director had been released from imprisonment for sedition on condition that he ceased all use of cameras. With infectious good humour, pretending to be a Tehran cab driver Panahi was filmed driving around town picking up and dropping shared fares, in friendly talk, eyes sparkling behind angular spectacles below a flat grey cap. Near the beginning an older woman holding tight in both hands a glass bowl with a goldfish swimming around inside, on its way to cathartic release in a holy spring, left by mistake her purse behind on the back seat. At the end of the film Panahi, the pretend taxi driver, found the large lady at down-town's traditional water garden and returned her missing possessions. *Ten* was similarly structured around conversations between a taxi driver and her passengers, though more overtly political. The old woman in Kiarostami's film was less benign in her superstitions than the goldfish lady in Panahi's, wastefully committed to catching a cab three times every single day to pray at the mausoleum where her husband and son were buried. Brian wondered how they had died, and realized that this may have been a detail he missed with his suspect eyesight, or perhaps through the impossibility accurately to transfer the full Iranian dialogue into the subtitles – which, anyway, he could not properly read.

On his way out of the cinema Brian found himself puzzling as to where the camera could have been concealed in the Panahi film, indeed in the Kiarostami too. At the door he slapped his forehead, ordering himself not to be such an idiot and spoil the fun by trying to work everything out.

Jafar Panahi's film in particular was just such a joy. That was what mattered.

Other films were a misery. Without informed notes available in time for the preview of Mike Leigh's *Peterloo* Brian felt lost, unfamiliar with its historical setting and unable always to hear above the shouted interruptions of the rural crowds what Orator Hunt said in his public speeches. Too many raucous market scenes and too much firing of rifles by men in red uniforms spread aural and visual chaos, ruining Brian's evening.

Bearing solitary strain for his deteriorating sight took its toll. Though his distancing from Jack was deliberate, Brian hated behaving as he did. It was hard also giving a convincing performance to the other buffs night after night – keeping the show on the road, he thought of it. Brian's stoop lowered, the bulge on his spine grew and his jowls drooped. Unable to fall asleep at night with worries running compulsively around his head, he dozed fitfully in the warmth and comfort of the BFI through passages in most films. There were moments on the way home, unable to recall the full narrative of the movie he had read up during the day and pretended to see that night, when he thought it best to reel straight to the credits.

Topple over the rail of Charing Cross Bridge into the winter-cold water, tide racing.

Drop beneath an oncoming Underground train at Embankment Station.

Step in front of a giant delivery lorry careering down Kentish Town Road at night.

He did none of these things.

When he got up from bed the next morning after the

worst sleepless night of his life and methodically made himself breakfast, he knew he was going to carry on as if everything was exactly as it always had been.

He looked sharply up at a knocking on the glass of the kitchen window, his scowl transforming into a smile at the sight of a small brown bird pecking insects from the moss on the wooden frame.

Research on each of the films he was due to see occupied the mornings, after which Brian renewed his Camden Housing Office habit of a late lunch every single day at Il Castelletto, where he often spent a couple of hours, reading, chatting to Lorenzo, and to Tony if he happened to be there. When Marian was in the mood, they shared a table and talked about their books of the week, intrigued by each other's radically different taste, Marian a traditionalist in essence, Brian avant garde by comparison. They used to swop quotes, Brian one day reading out published words by Christian Marclay, the clock video man:

> It's just like if you make a sound with a record and it skips
> in a certain way - those are interesting moments when
> you kind of lose control while you're trying to accomplish
> something. I think that's just life.

To which Marian responded with an entertaining but not obviously connected quote from the poet-painter William Blake: 'The man who never alters his opinion is like standing water, and breeds reptiles of the mind.'

Not knowing quite what to say to this, Brian glanced over for inspiration at the Tina picture hanging on the wall behind the counter. And still could not think of a response. Instead he smiled at Isabella, Lorenzo's daughter, in her A-Level year and working in the café in the school holidays to earn pocket money. Her youngest brother was in the youth squad at Leighton Orient, though with no intention, Lorenzo had said, of becoming a professional footballer, determined on a career in nursing.

Film still your thing, Brian? Lorenzo checked.

Of course. Did some research the other day on Japanese cinema for the British Film Institute.

Did you hear that, Maid M? That'll keep our Brian out of trouble now he's retired, Lorenzo said, winking at Marian.

As usual the menu at Il Castelletto was written in coloured chalks on a blackboard on the wall by the hatch to the basement kitchen. Although changes were infrequent, Brian consulted the board every day, partly to test his reading glasses, needing regular reassurance that it was only his distance vision which had gone haywire.

After lunch, if confident about his preparation for the evening's films, Brian sometimes went home for an afternoon nap, or occasionally walked over to the Jewish Museum in nearby Albert Street, refurbished with an attractive café and research centre, where they had inherited a select body of material on film.

By learning to hear moods and messages in the sounds and scores of an increasing number of the new movies with nominal dialogue, Brian felt sufficiently informed to contribute helpfully to the buffs' post-screen discussions. He came to trust that though the content of his comments had changed, their relevance remained consistent. If anybody noticed the difference they did not say, in the usual way of the regulars, sensitive to each other's vulnerability. In time Brian managed almost to forget that he had once watched the films he now largely listened to. He knew that his learning to hear and interpret sound in film had largely grown from Jack's friendship and his generous sharing of knowledge on movie scores.

In a self-set test, Brian was nervous about for the first time seeing – about not seeing, to be accurate – *My Dinner with Andre*, the Louis Malle movie made over thirty years before, in which two friends sat down for dinner in a fashionable Manhattan restaurant. And talked. Nothing else, for two hours. Brian was afraid of missing the significant message in an unclearly seen by him raised eyebrow or false smile, and of misinterpreting the meaning of a plainly heard choked-back laugh, only hazily able to spot the visual context. From the films by Malle he had watched some time ago, Brian knew that he was a teasing director, a wealthy Catholic unconcerned for the box office success of his work, prepared to tackle taboo subjects and take cinematic risks.

Brian was ready, therefore, to be confused.

He need not have worried. The rhythm of conversation between the theatre director André Gregory and writer Wallace Shawn, playing undramatic versions of themselves, was maybe better heard than seen, the playful exchange of suspect ideas saved from the distraction of perceiving in full the background antics of a louche waiter or being diverted by the historic photographs and pictures hanging on the walls of the Parisian style New York restaurant. There was also the score to listen to, composed by Wallace's brother Allen Shawn, appropriately traditional in form, given the main dish of roast quail and Satie's piano music interposed over the glass-clinking of dinner.

Brian felt so at ease at the buffs' post-film gathering that he dropped his prepared use of a quote, the exasperated remark in Wally Shawn's high-pitched voice near the end of the movie: 'I don't know what you're talking about!'

Nor do I, Brian had been planning to add, redundant

now after feeling that he had managed to take in the essential nature of *My Dinner with Andre*.

He had survived existential shocks. His world of film had not disintegrated. And his public stand was not a lie, not really, not even a disguise, more like a scripted change of costume. Brian felt proud of himself and decided to buy Jack a Christmas present in gratitude for his loyalty, a thank-you for sticking it out without saying anything and waiting for him to find his own path forward.

The experience of choosing, buying and wrapping a present was a novelty, something Brian had not done as an adult, for anyone. The last time he had bought a Christmas present was for his mother, when he was sixteen, a tin-opener as theirs at home in Rochester had disappeared.

They were always losing things.

His mother gave him the year's Disneyland Annual, gift-wrapped by Woolworth's. She had died three weeks later.

He still owned the book, now in a clear protective plastic jacket to show off the cartoon drawing on the front cover, of Donald Duck and Mickey Mouse at play in a blow-up rubber boat.

Predictably, Brian changed his mind a dozen times about the best present to get for his friend – nothing excessive, ideally something Jack might have bought for himself, if he had thought of it and had the money. After a couple of dispiriting afternoons trudging around the Oxford Street shops, wearing his trenchcoat against the weather, Brian decided on a roll-neck sweater of sage green Donegal wool, from Liberty's on Regent Street, more expensive than he had intended but something he was certain Jack would like. Of lasting quality, up to the heavy wear Jack gave his clothes. From W.H.Smith in Kentish Town Road on the way home from the tube station he bought a pack of thick brown paper, wrapped the sweater safely in two layers, sellotaped the folded corners and addressed the package in capital letters to Jack in Tooting. In order to silence the clamour of doubt Brian walked straight round to the Post Office and dispatched the present.

No note. No sender's address.

No Happy Christmas and Prosperous New Year.

This was the only way Brian could persuade himself, after fifty-four years of never giving a gift, now to do so. Anonymously, leaving it up to Jack to set the consequences in motion if he wished.

Jack might suspect that it was a dishonourable breaking by one or other of the buffs of the habit of personal distance and choose to say nothing. He might think and hope it was from a particular somebody else, from his non-film life. He might not be bothered to work it out either way, put on the sweater without delay and seldom be seen wearing anything else for months.

Just possibly Jack might follow the clues of NW1 postmark and Irish green, put two and two together and be pleased.

Brian was content to be patient and wait.

If nothing happened, when the right time came he intended to let Jack know that the present was from him.